JL MERROW

LOVERS LEAP

RIPTIDE
PUBLISHING

Riptide Publishing
PO Box 1537
Burnsville, NC 28714
www.riptidepublishing.com

Lovers Leap

Cover art: Lou Harper, louharper.com/design.html
Editor: Kate de Groot
Layout: L.C. Chase, lcchase.com/design.htm

ISBN: 978-1-62649-383-4

First edition
February, 2016

Also available in ebook:
ISBN: 978-1-62649-382-7

JL MERROW

LOVERS LEAP

RIPTIDE
PUBLISHING

With thanks to Kristin, Susan Sorrentino, and Josephine Myles. And with apologies to Sandown Pier, which I'm sure is entirely safe and well maintained. But honestly, people who go larking about near the water shouldn't be surprised if they get a dunking!

TABLE OF CONTENTS

CHAPTER I
DIVE

Michael stomped along Sandown Pier, his footsteps loud on the wooden boards. The salt-laden wind was blowing right through him, last night's beer had left him with a headache, and Trix was *still talking*. He should never have agreed to come on this holiday—for God's sake, who went to the Isle of Wight in February? Far as he was concerned, there was bugger all romantic about freezing your balls off, and it wasn't even like it was Valentine's Day. That'd been over two weeks ago.

It was time he ended this. *Way* past time. It just wasn't working. Couldn't she see that? Michael wasn't even certain he was really that into girls, if he was honest with himself, which as a rule he tried not to be.

Trix had seemed all right when she turned up at his kickboxing club a few weeks ago and they started sparring—she'd punched harder than any girl he'd met, and she had a kick like a pissed-off mule. So he'd invited her out to run with him one Saturday morning, which had ended in some X-rated shower action back at hers. She'd taken him mountain biking, which wasn't really his thing, but getting frisky in the forest . . . Yeah, he could get behind that. He was bi, she was bi; it was like they were made for each other, right? Perfect for a bit of fun. But the trouble was, when they'd got on the ferry, he'd found out that once she had her breath back, she just never stopped *talking*.

Michael was sick of trying to tune it out. He'd been hanging around hoping she'd get the message and dump him, but enough was enough. Time to cut his losses and head on home. "Sorry, love, but we gotta split up," he said, not waiting for her to finish what she was saying because he was twenty-six already and he might not live that long.

Trix stared at him, her mouth hanging open and silent for once, and backed off a few steps. "Hey, careful there," Michael said, cos they'd reached the concrete bit at the end of the pier, where boats could pull in or park or whatever boats did, and the railings were pretty low.

Then what she'd just been saying finally percolated through his brain: *"Michael, babes, I love you so much, will you marry me?"*

"Uh . . ." he started.

She didn't give him a chance to get any further. Her cherry-red lips drawn up in a snarl, she ran at him.

Caught unprepared, Michael didn't offer any resistance as she gave him a bloody great shove with ten stone of kickboxing muscle behind it. His lower back hit the rail, 'cept it wasn't a proper rail on this side, just a bit of old chain. It swung taut—and then something gave way, and it wasn't taut anymore, and he was falling.

Right off the end of the pier.

CHAPTER 2
SURGE

It was a bit nippy that day, and Rufus wrapped his wool coat tighter around himself as he promenaded down the beach and under the barnacle-encrusted supports of Sandown Pier, master of all he surveyed. Well, technically not master of all or, in fact, *any* of it, but there was no one around to challenge his claim, so he could pretend it was all his.

Mostly, obviously, it was sand, but that was all right. Rufus would never forget the first time he went to Brighton and was horrified by that quarry pit they had the nerve to call a beach there. No, as the name might tend to imply, they had *proper* beaches in Sandown. Which was just as well, as some might say there wasn't much else to shout about, particularly in the winter, when the hotels and most of the shops were shut up for the off-season. Rufus, however, liked to think there was a certain desolate charm to the place.

At any rate, if you wanted to go for a solitary walk on your birthday, and said birthday happened to be at the end of February, you could pretty much guarantee you wouldn't be overwhelmed by seething throngs of people on the beach.

It was only the fifth real birthday he'd had, having been born twenty years ago on leap day, February 29. Some people considered it unlucky, but Rufus preferred to think of it as special. Unusual things could happen on a day that only came around once every four years. After all, *he'd* happened on a leap day, and people were always telling him he was special, although he had a strong suspicion they didn't necessarily mean it in a good way.

Today, his firm belief in the specialness of leap days was amply justified.

There was a man walking out of the sea towards him, just like Daniel Craig in *Casino Royale*, only he wasn't wearing little blue trunks, which, given the current temperature, was probably just as well. No, he was fully clothed and sopping wet in the biting wind.

Rufus stared at the man, wondering whether, in the face of this unexpected birthday present, he ought to reconsider his halfhearted Church of England agnosticism and convert to worshipping Poseidon. And whether the sea god would expect him to sacrifice his firstborn in gratitude, which was likely to prove something of a problem, what with him being gay and all.

Rufus's unexpected gift from the gods was tall and nicely broad-shouldered, with a fair bit of muscle—not all of that bulk was due to the Puffa jacket dripping from his shoulders. Dark-haired, although it was probably a bit lighter when it wasn't plastered to his head with seawater. His eyes were the blue of the bay on a sunny day. Unlike the dull, muddy green it was on this particular day, which was more the colour of *Rufus's* eyes. He was gorgeous, this bloke was, in a rough-diamond, macho-man way. He had the kind of looks you'd expect to see on the face of someone brandishing a cutlass and demanding you give up your booty.

Rufus was ready to give it up all right. No question. This man was *literally* a wet dream, and he was walking straight towards Rufus.

Could he be a selkie? Rufus briefly considered the possibility of seal-shifters (a) being real and (b) bothering to turn up on the Isle of Wight. In February. Yeah, get real. Anyway, from the pissed-off expression, this bloke looked like more of a sulkie.

"You're late," Rufus said, unable to stop himself.

The wet man frowned. Wetly. "You what?"

"You're late. The New Year's Day swim was two months ago. And, just so you know, they usually wear actual swimming gear."

One dark eyebrow lifted a bit, causing a trickle of seawater to run a little more quickly down his face. He grimaced and swiped at it with one huge paw. "That what you're hanging around here for? To ogle the blokes in their Speedos?"

"No, obviously, because *I* know what month it is." Rufus paused, but it didn't look like he was about to get beaten up in this *precise* moment. And he was fairly sure he'd be able to run faster than the man in front of him, what with all those wet clothes weighing him down.

"So is that what you're wearing under that lot? Speedos?"

"You wish." Then he shivered. "Christ, it's colder than a witch's tit in a brass bra. You live round here?"

Rufus nodded. "Yeah. Not far. Queen Street. My parents have got a B&B." He swallowed, because this was starting to seem like it might be about to turn into one of his dreams or a porno or something (not a lot of difference, if he was honest, most of the time). Was this the bit where the wet guy winked at him and said, *Come on then, don't you want to get me out of these wet clothes?*

What the wet guy *actually* did was scowl and say, "Well? You just gonna stand there and watch me die of hypothermia, or are you gonna get me somewhere warm?"

Close enough.

"All right, it's this way. Rufus," he added. "I mean, that's me. Rufus Kewell."

The man gave him the usual disbelieving look.

"Yes, yes, I know. Mum saw Rufus Sewell in *Middlemarch* and got *totally* besotted. Had a signed photo on her bedside table and everything, which I think Dad was *amazingly* understanding about. Bit of a shame I don't look anything like him. Rufus Sewell, that is, not Dad. Apart from the height, of course. And the eyes. And the cheekbones, maybe, although actually I think mine are better than his. But as you can see, I'm totally blond. And he's not."

The look went on a little longer. "Michael," the stranger said at last. "Talk a lot, don't you?"

Rufus nodded. Couldn't argue with that. "Are you here on holiday? Sorry, stupid question." It had just popped out automatically, like the way if someone said they liked their coffee strong, you always felt you had to ask, *Like your men?* Well, Rufus did, anyway. "Who comes to the Isle of Wight on holiday in February?" he asked rhetorically, with a self-deprecating laugh.

"Me, actually. With my girlfriend."

Well, there had only been a *very* small chance he'd be gay, Rufus thought philosophically, although if Poseidon thought he'd be getting any sacrifices now, he was very much mistaken.

Michael glanced back at the pier. "Ex-girlfriend," he amended. Then he laughed.

Rufus perked up. Then he perked straight back down again, because even an *ex*-girlfriend probably meant Michael wouldn't be up for having a *boy*friend, and even if he *was* up for it, he didn't live locally. But god, he was hot. Like everyone's favourite dark and brooding hero, but with an extra dollop of dark and a great big barrelful of brood.

"Do you want to come to mine and get dry?" Rufus asked hopefully, because even if, as was almost certainly the case, nothing would come of it, he'd still stand a very good chance of getting an eyeful.

On the Isle of Wight in winter, you had to take your pleasures where you could find them.

Michael gave him a withering look. "Does a hobbyhorse have a wooden dick?"

"Not in my experience, no," Rufus said politely. "Big childhood disappointment, actually. But I'll take that as a yes."

He led the way along the Esplanade, deserted but for a few dog walkers and an elderly couple, who paused their bent-backed amble to stare myopically as Michael squelched past. "You'll catch your death," the old lady tutted helpfully.

"Christ, how far is this place?" Michael muttered.

"Not far. Just up the slipway, past the trampolines—at least, there aren't any there *now*, but if it was summer, there would be—and we're almost there."

"Jesus. You ever try to walk this far in wet jeans? My bollocks are gonna be rubbed raw by the time we get there."

Should Rufus offer to kiss them better?

He side-eyed Michael's broad, muscular shoulders and large, capable fists. Probably not *quite* this soon in their relationship.

The small car park outside the Eldorado B&B was empty, which was good, as it meant Rufus's dad and stepmum were still out and therefore unable to ask awkward questions, such as why Rufus was bringing a soaking-wet stranger into the house.

Although come to think of it, they'd probably just put it down to him being Rufus.

"This way," he said. He led Michael around to the side and let him into their large, well-equipped kitchen. The front door, with its Victorian fanlight and antique bell push, was for guests. Meaning paying guests.

Rufus's room was upstairs on the first floor, one of the poky ones round the back. Well, that was his room during the summer season. *Officially*, in the winter, he had the nice big room at the front with the bay window, but he hadn't quite got round to moving his stuff in there yet this year.

Given that they had bookings for the Easter school holidays, he was beginning to suspect he might have left it a tiny bit too late to bother.

Michael looked around. It didn't take him long. "Bloody hell, it's like a sodding shoebox with a bed in it. I've seen abandoned kittens with better accommodation than this. Your mum and dad not like you, or what?"

"It's cosy," Rufus said firmly. "Don't drip on the duvet."

"What am I supposed to do with my kit, then? Hang it out the window?" He'd got his jacket off and dumped it on the floor, and was peeling off his sweater, which looked a bit sad and saggy. "Shit. I like this jumper."

"Maybe it'll come up all right in the wash?" Rufus hazarded. "You get all your stuff off, and I'll bung it in the machine."

"Yeah, and then what? Not like I'm gonna fit into anything of yours, is it?" He was down to his jeans now, pulling his see-through T-shirt over his head as he spoke, to display a darkly haired, muscular chest that, yes, was likely to prove a challenge to any of Rufus's T-shirts.

Rufus paused for a moment, pretending to be deep in thought while he gazed his fill. "I'll get you one of my dad's shirts. He won't mind." Well, he probably wouldn't notice, which came to the same thing.

Unfortunately, this meant Rufus had to leave the room right when Michael was undoing his jeans. Fortunately, this meant that when he got back to his bedroom, Michael was standing there stark bollock naked.

He had one foot up on the bed and a hand holding his junk out of the way while he peered at his inner thigh. "Christ, look at that. Rubbed fucking raw."

Rufus swallowed, and looked. Well, he'd been invited to. It was only polite. "Yeah, that does look a bit sore. I could get some Savlon cream?" he suggested.

"Nah, I'm not that much of a wuss." Michael let go of his junk and took his foot off the bed. His cock fell, thick and long, between his muscular (and slightly chafed) thighs, in front of a pair of heavy, thickly furred bollocks.

Rufus probably should have realised Michael was giving him a funny look, but in his defence, he was a bit distracted.

"Oi. Are you perving on my dick?"

Rufus's face, which, let's—hah—face it, had been feeling pretty warm already, went red-hot. "No." It was possibly the least convincing lie he'd ever told. In a long, sad line of unconvincing lies that went all the way back to "No, I never play with dollies."

"You're perving on my dick, aren't you? Jesus. Here I am, only seconds away from near-death of hypothermia, chafed so bad I practically need a skin graft, and you're perving on my bloody dick."

That was totally unfair. Rufus wasn't just perving on his *dick*.

"I could take you back down to the beach and throw you back in, you know," Rufus muttered sullenly.

Michael laughed. "You and whose army, pretty boy?"

Rufus bristled. "I could be a master of jujitsu."

"No, you couldn't," Michael said, although it sounded kindly as well as scornful. "That oriental stuff's all style and no fucking substance, anyhow. Show me any black belt, any discipline you like, I bet I could beat him in a fight."

"What are you, some kind of ninja?"

"Nah. Kickboxer. So are you gonna give me that shirt or what?"

"Oh. Sorry." Rufus handed it over, resolving to avoid all unwanted perving from now on. He'd never been kickboxed. He was fairly sure he didn't want to start now. "You know what's good for hypothermia?" he couldn't help adding. So much for that resolution.

Michael gave him a look. "Is this where you offer me skin-on-skin contact to get my temperature up? What do you think this is? Some kind of gay porno?"

Rufus swallowed. "Um, no?"

Michael stepped closer. "Do you want it to be?"

Oh *god*, yes. "Um. See, this is the sort of question I might have to think about. I mean, you just told me you're a kickboxer, and you came here with your girlfriend, so what I'm *really* asking is, if I say yes, is it going to get me laid, or is it going to get me—"

"Shut up," Michael said, not too roughly, and kissed him.

CHAPTER 3
JERK

Michael knew he was being a shit. But Christ, the kid was just asking for it, in more ways than one. Standing there staring at Michael's dick with his tongue hanging out between those pretty red lips. And it wasn't like Michael was gonna be getting any from Trix tonight, or any other night come to that, so why not show the kid a good time?

Jesus, how old was he, anyway? He knew how to kiss, but that meant sod all. "You legal?" Michael asked, taking a regretful step back. He was already getting hard just from that brief contact, and he'd have liked the opportunity to get even harder, ta very much.

"I'm twenty," the kid squeaked, his gaze fixed firmly to Michael's rising dick like it held all the secrets of the universe.

Yeah, right. "No fucking way."

Rufus smirked. "*Way.*" Jesus, he was cute when he was being cheeky. Then he had to ruin it. "Although it is my fifth birthday today. I thought at first you were my present. I mean, I did get to unwrap you."

Fucking marvellous. Michael might be a shit, but even he drew the line at screwing anyone without the mental capacity to consent. He sighed and started pulling on the borrowed shirt, his dick deflating rapidly.

Rufus stared at him with big, wide eyes that seemed brown one minute and green the next. "What did I say?"

"Look, you're cute, yeah? But you probably oughtta just sit tight and wait for your carer to get back."

"No, no—wait." Rufus grabbed hold of Michael's arm, as if he thought Michael was actually going anywhere dressed in nothing but a borrowed old-man shirt with his dick hanging out. "See here? My driving licence. Date of birth, 29 February 1996. So I'm twenty, yeah, but it's my fifth birthday. I'm a leapling. And a caulkhead, meaning I was born on the island, but that's kind of not relevant right—*mmph*."

Michael had stopped listening after "1996." His dick chubbing up again nicely, he yanked Rufus back against him and carried on with that kiss. Yeah, that was good. He dropped his hands to grab a couple of handfuls of firm little arse. Fuck, yeah. He was having that. "You got condoms?" he breathed into Rufus's ear.

"Um. Yes?" Rufus looked around the room like he thought they were gonna jump out of a drawer and throw themselves at him. "Somewhere—"

"Don't bother." Michael's dick just didn't have the patience. And while he might've been kicked out of the Boy Scouts at age eleven, he was *always* prepared. He grabbed his sodden jeans and felt in the back pocket. Yep, condom and lube. Good thing they came foil wrapped. "You need much prep?"

"Um."

"You've done anal before, right?"

"Yes! Lots of times."

Rufus might as well have had a big red neon sign above his head, flashing *LIE*. Michael sighed. This *really* wasn't his day. "Look, you can just suck me off, okay?"

"No! I mean, yes, but . . . I want to. Do, you know. Anal. I really, *really* want to. It's leap year, right? Time to try something new."

"Ever had anything up there?"

Rufus nodded—then dived under the bed. He came back with a large shoebox, which he opened. "See?"

Yeah, Michael saw, all right. It was kinda hard to miss a bright-purple dildo, especially one of that size. He was grudgingly impressed.

Also starting to feel a bit inadequate, but bugger that.

No, wait. He focused back on Rufus's pert little arse. Bugger *that*. He smiled. "Better get your kit off, then." Still kneeling on the floor—and Michael had *zero* problem with that—Rufus stripped off his sweater and T-shirt together, revealing a slender, hairless torso, not bulky but lean. Nice. "You work out?"

Rufus blushed. "I do yoga."

Michael grinned. "Bendy little fucker, are you?"

There was that cheeky smile again. "*Oh* yeah." Rufus stood up, undid his jeans, and pushed them and his boxer briefs off in one quick motion. Then he climbed onto the bed and lay back, grinning at Michael from between legs that were spread wide, his feet pointing to the ceiling and his hands around his ankles. His dick, which sprouted from a nest of neatly trimmed blond fuzz, was fucking perfect—hard, leaking, and just a little bit smaller than Michael's.

Shit. Michael was in love. He scrambled onto the bed and grabbed hold of that arse with both hands. "Fuck me. You're gonna feel this for *weeks*."

Rufus's eyes opened wider, and the grin faltered a bit, but he didn't move. "I can take anything you can give me."

"Cocky sod. Let's see how you like this." Kneeling, Michael smoothed on the condom with the speed of one hell of a lot of practice, lubed up his fingers, and shoved in two at once—slowly, cos he wasn't a total bastard.

Rufus's eyes rolled up in his head. "Oh god."

"Plenty more where that came from." Michael added another finger, pinching a nipple with his other hand to take the kid's mind off any possible discomfort. He was thoughtful like that.

"Oh god," Rufus said again. Then, "Oh *god*," as Michael hit the magic button inside him. His whole body jerked, his dick leaking a sticky trail onto his belly.

Michael pulled out his fingers and slapped some more lube on his cock. "Ready for this?" Because Christ, Michael was. His dick was so full and hard he felt light-headed from the lack of blood to the brain.

"Yes, god, yes . . ." Rufus's eager babbling was a sweet little boost to the ego.

Michael pushed inside. Jesus, that arse was *perfect*. Hot and tight, it grabbed hold of his dick and lured him into virgin territory, and Michael wasn't gonna pretend that wasn't an extra thrill. You always remembered your first, right? Michael was gonna make this one to tell the grandkids about.

Well. Maybe not literally.

He groaned as he bottomed out, hips pressed to Rufus's arse. So fucking good.

Rufus was staring at Michael like he was the fucking Holy Grail.

"All right there?" Michael asked, a bit short of breath.

Rufus didn't answer, still staring at Michael wide-eyed and openmouthed.

"Oi," Michael prompted, with a gentle slap to Rufus's arse. The vibration travelled through to his dick and felt pretty good, so he did it again just for fun. "You okay there?"

"Yes, god," Rufus blurted out. "*Please* move."

Michael laughed. "Only cos you asked so nicely." He pulled out almost all the way, then slowly thrust back in, drawing a long, low groan from Rufus that gave Michael the shivers and had the added bonus of covering up his own moan. Jesus, that felt good. "Ready to go up a gear?"

Rufus nodded frantically.

Michael let go. He pounded Rufus's arse harder and harder, his balls slapping against skin with a rhythmic *thwack*. Jesus, this wasn't gonna last—

Rufus's face went from slack-jawed pleasure to screwed-up ecstasy as he shot all over his own chest, dick untouched, gasping out some weird bloke's name—P'Simon?—but Michael didn't give a monkey's cos he could finally, *finally* let go. With a groan of relief so loud they must have heard it back on the mainland, Michael emptied his balls into that tight little body.

Panting hard, Michael stayed where he was until the last of the aftershocks had died away. Then, before the lethargy could hit, he grabbed the base of the condom and pulled out. Fuck, that had been awesome. He stripped off the condom and dropped it on the floor, then gave Rufus a sloppy kiss.

"Got a pen?" he asked, his voice coming out breathless.

Still looking dazed, Rufus scrabbled around in his bedside drawer. "Pen, pen . . . Yes. Here you go."

"Right. C'mere." Michael grabbed Rufus's face with both hands, kissed him one last time, then scribbled down his phone number on Rufus's forehead. "Next time you're in Southampton, gimme a call and we'll do this again."

He gave Rufus the pen back, tugged on his still-wet jeans— *Fuck, that's gross*—grabbed his jacket from its sodden puddle on the floor, jammed his feet into his trainers—*Jesus, that's even worse*—and squelched away.

CHAPTER 4
BOB

Rufus was left lying on the bed, staring at the door, his chest wet with spunk and his head in a whirl. He felt changed, different. No longer a virgin—not that he hadn't fooled around before, but no one could ever say he hadn't had proper sex now.

He'd heard the first time was always supposed to be crap, something to get out of the way before you met the bloke of your dreams, cos you didn't want to start a perfect relationship with rubbish sex. But that had been *amazing*. He could hardly believe big, scary Michael had been so gentle with him. Even when he was being rough. Did that make sense? Oh, who cared. It'd been *perfect*.

It felt like a dream. Had it even happened? He moved, and felt a twinge in his arse that said yes, yes it had. And when he got out of bed, his carpet was wet, there was a definite whiff of seawater in the air underneath the reek of sex, and as a clincher, the mirror above the tiny washbasin in his room showed an eleven-figure number scrawled on his forehead. Rufus looked at the pen still in his hand.

It was a permanent marker.

Oh, buggering *bollocks*.

Rufus ran the tap until the water was scalding, squirted out a generous dollop of soap, and scrubbed furiously at his forehead. *Shit, shit . . . Shit.* He hadn't made a note of the number first. Oh god. Rufus closed his eyes in despair. The most gorgeous bloke he'd ever met, the best shag he'd ever had—technically, the *only* shag he'd ever had—and he'd just washed away his one means of getting back in touch.

He was an *idiot*.

Rufus opened his eyes to glare at himself in the mirror. And realised the number was still there, only marginally fainter than before. Thank Poseidon.

He grabbed a piece of paper and painstakingly wrote down the number, double- and triple-checking to make sure he hadn't got any digits round the wrong way. Then he put it straight into his phone just to make certain.

Then he switched off his phone and put it in his bedside drawer. Just in case his fingers might slip, hit Call, and propel him straight into needy clingy stalker territory. Three days—that was the minimum time before calling, wasn't it? Or was it two now, what with shorter attention spans these days? If he left it too long, Michael would be back in Southampton. He might be on his way back there already. Maybe a quick text right now wouldn't hurt . . . Rufus found his hands straying towards the drawer and folded his arms quickly to keep them in line.

Of course, that just left him back at square one—with a bloody great phone number written on his head. Maybe if he combed his hair forward? Yeah, and spent a couple of months growing it first. Rufus sighed. Camouflage. It was the only option. Baseball cap pulled low? That might work.

If he owned a baseball cap. Hm. Beanie? He had one of those. Except Dad would ask him why he was wearing it in the house.

Rufus had to think fast. They could be home at any minute. He sprayed on some deodorant, sprayed a bit around the room for good measure, pulled on his clothes, and sneaked into Dad and Shelley's room on tiptoe. Even when they were out, he instinctively felt sneaking was essential. It had been a total no-go area for him after they first got together—he'd definitely come to appreciate the usefulness of earplugs that first summer—and even two years later it gave him a weird feeling going in there. But maybe Dad still had that old 1970s-style tennis sweatband . . . No, wait. This was even better.

He grabbed one of Shelley's animal-print scarves from the loopy thing that hung on the wall and tied the wispy fabric around his head. Then he peered at himself in her dressing-table mirror, the view a bit fuzzy because she liked to put on lots of bronzing powder with a big floofy brush and hated dusting. Hm. Maybe not the leopard. The zebra?

Yes. Yes, that was much better. Much manlier.

He went downstairs to put the kettle on. As he finished filling it, Dad and Shelley walked in.

Rufus had a moment of panic—would they be able to tell, simply by looking at him, what had happened? But no, that was ridiculous. Just cos he *felt* different didn't mean he looked it.

"Happy birthday, love!" Shelley said with a big smile, and came to give him a hug, although she'd done both already, first thing this morning. Dad had probably told her his last birthday, when he'd been sixteen, had been a little bit crap, what with Mum dying of cancer. Not on the *day*, because even Rufus's luck wasn't that shitty all of the time, but soon after. So she was probably trying to make up for that. Well, and for not being Rufus's real mum, although he was never quite sure why she seemed to think that needed making up for. After all, it wasn't *her* fault.

Dad, being his real parent, just nodded at him. "Had fun with your presents?" he asked gruffly.

Rufus froze guiltily, before realising that of course Dad meant his *actual* presents, which had been a beautiful red and black Vitamix blender and a blowtorch that came with its own little set of cute porcelain ramekins. Not, say, any bits of rough trade that might have been washed up on Sandown beach. "I'm saving it for tonight. I thought I'd do duck with a Pinot and raspberry jus, served with potato and tarragon rosti, and followed, obviously, by orange crème brûlée."

Their eyes glazed over like ham cooked in honey and marmalade. Rufus frequently got the feeling they weren't really into it when he talked menus.

"You know," Dad said a bit hesitantly. "The offer still stands if you want to go out for a meal instead."

"Yeah, love," Shelley put in, hanging on to Dad's arm. "You sure you want to cook on your birthday? You wouldn't catch me doing that."

Rufus was way too tactful to point out it was pretty hard to catch Shelley cooking on any of the other three hundred and sixty-four-stroke-five days of the year, either. But Dad had the decency to look embarrassed. Last time *he'd* been caught with a spatula in his hand, he'd been looking for something to help him even out the grout on the guests' bathroom tiles.

Shelley was staring at him, a frown on her carefully made-up face. Oh god—*could* she tell what he'd been up to? Did he look different after all? More mature? Less innocent? Totally shagged?

"Rufus, love? Why have you got one of my scarves tied around your head?"

Oh. That. If he crossed his fingers, she might see, so Rufus surreptitiously crossed his toes inside his Crocs. "I, um, thought it might make me look more butch. Like Rambo, you know, in Dad's old DVDs? Is it working?"

"Cup of tea, anyone?" Dad said quickly.

Shelley grabbed on to that lifeline with both hands. "Ooh, that'd be lovely, ta."

Rufus guessed that was a no, then. "Never mind. Maybe the butchness quotient will increase once I've worn it in. You don't mind me borrowing it, do you, Shelley?"

"Course not, love. I know what it's like when you're young. You never have enough stuff. Me and my sister used to share clothes all the time. You miss out on that, being an only child."

Dad coughed. "Lads don't tend to do that sort of thing."

"Sez you." Shelley kissed Dad on the cheek. Sweet, but *ew*. "Maybe not when *you* were a lad. I bet boys of Rufus's age do it all the time."

"No, we're all too busy playing FPS games on our Xboxes and mugging old ladies while dressed in hoodies," Rufus contradicted her with a fond smile. He liked Shelley, probably because she never tried to actually be a mum to him. "And Dad? FPS means first-person shooter, and an Xbox is a—"

"You know, you're not too big for me to put you over my knee," Dad interrupted with a mock glare.

"I'm not sure about that," Rufus said seriously. "I wouldn't want you to strain anything."

Before Dad could respond, there was a loud banging on the side door. Shelley frowned. "I wonder who on earth that could be?"

Rufus was wondering too. Friends tended to just open the door and yell, and the postman had been already. It couldn't be Michael, could it? He wiped suddenly sweaty palms on his jeans and told himself not to be stupid. Guys who said, *"Gimme a call next time you're in Southampton"* and wrote their number on your forehead—in *permanent marker*—weren't the sort to come back half an hour later because they missed you already.

Although Michael had left his sweater behind. And his T-shirt, and his briefs. Rufus had been planning to hang them up to dry and keep them forever as a memento. Possibly wrapped around his dildo . . .

Rufus was startled out of his reverie when Shelley pushed back her chair and went to open the door.

CHAPTER 5
PLUMMET

Michael must have looked a right sight, walking up the high street in wet jeans and an old-man shirt, carrying a dripping-wet jacket. Shit, he'd left his sweater behind. Not to mention his underwear.

He'd had to get away, though. Wouldn't have been a good idea to hang around, get too cosy. That sort of thing led to feelings and stuff, and Michael didn't get feelings for pretty little boys—okay, maybe not so little, but fuck, he was pretty—who could never, not in a million years, be explained away as just a mate. Michael's mates were all like him: lads' lads. Blokes who liked a pint or six and a game of footie, preferably at the same time. Blokes who knew their way around an engine, who didn't bother with all this metrosexual male grooming shit, and who you could count on in a fight.

Straight blokes.

Because Michael wasn't gay, yeah? He was bi, which meant he did what he wanted, fooled around with guys as well as girls, but that was all it was. He didn't have *relationships*. Not with guys. Not much with girls—and that business with Trix had only gone to show how sensible that was—but definitely not with guys. One day, when he was ready, he'd find a girl he liked well enough, and make his mum happy by getting married. But Christ, not yet.

Shit, wet jeans were a *bitch*.

He needed to get back to the hotel him and Trix were staying in. Maybe he could patch things up with her? They still had the rest of the week booked. Nah, what was he thinking? Even if she weren't still mad at him, she'd only want to *talk* about it. Course, might be worth it for the make-up sex . . . 'cept every time he tried to picture getting

Trix naked, she turned into Rufus the minute he got her kit off. What the hell?

Jesus, it was just as well he hadn't hung around there any longer. The last thing he needed was some pretty boy with a hot body messing with his head.

Finally, he reached the hotel. The blonde receptionist who'd been so friendly when they checked in on Friday night—Michael reckoned she fancied him, and bollocks to what Trix had said about it just being cos they were the only guests—was busy with something, so Michael didn't bother with a greeting. Probably best she didn't notice him walking by in such a state.

"Mr. O'Grady? *Mr. O'Grady*," she called out after him just as he was about to go up the stairs.

Sod it.

"Oh, uh, hi, Judy," he said, turning reluctantly. "What can I do you for?"

Her mouth was set in a thin pastel-pink line. "I've got your bag behind the counter, and you owe us for three nights. Miss Horton has already checked out, but she said you'd be in to settle the bill."

"Hang on a minute—Trix has gone?"

"Yes." Judy folded her arms across the front of her fluffy sweater. "She warned us you might be looking a little . . . disreputable when you came back."

Shit. "What else did she tell you?"

She ignored him. "Will you be paying by cash or credit card?"

"Look, hang on, the room's booked for a week, right? So let me go up and change, maybe stay another night or two"—he could always pay Rufus another visit—"and I'll check out when I'm ready."

"I'm sorry, Mr. O'Grady. I'm afraid the hotel has a strict policy of not accepting bookings from your sort."

Michael's hackles rose. "What the hell do you mean, 'my sort'?"

She smiled sweetly. "Arseholes."

Shit. Of *course* Trix had told her everything. "Look, I'm soaking wet, here. At least let me go up and get changed."

"I'm sorry, but rooms are only for the use of our guests. Your bag." She picked it up with an expression of disgust and dropped it over the counter.

Michael winced. Up until that moment he'd been glad he'd forgotten to take his phone with him. "I could strip off right here," he threatened.

"Certainly, if you'd like to get arrested for indecent exposure."

She had him there. Especially seeing as he'd left his kecks with Rufus. "What the hell am I supposed to do, then?"

"If you go back down the high street and turn right, you'll find some public toilets on the slipway. I'm sure you'll be able to manage there." Judy tapped long Barbie-pink talons on the counter. "Now, cash or credit card, Mr. O'Grady?"

Michael cursed—under his breath, cos she'd probably have him arrested for *that*—and pulled out his wallet. It hadn't fared any better than the rest of him, and the stack of twenty-pound notes inside was now one sodden mass. "Credit card," he ground out.

"Thank you, sir. You'll notice the total's left blank for you to fill in your own gratuity."

Gritting his teeth, Michael just about managed not to tear the slip as he filled in a big, fat zero.

He ought to be a candidate for bloody *sainthood* for that little bit of restraint.

Trudging down the high street, his bag slung over his shoulder, Michael considered his options. They'd come in Trix's Jeep, so he'd have to get a taxi to the ferry. And shit, what if he got on the same one as Trix? Swimming back to land from the end of the pier was one thing—for a start, the tide had been out, so he'd been able to walk most of the way. He didn't much fancy being dumped in the middle of the Solent and having to swim a couple of miles back to dry land. On the other hand . . . if he turned left instead of right when he got to the slipway, he could go back to Rufus's B&B.

Yeah. Yeah, that'd be the thing to do. He could get changed, could even pick up his sweater and offload this fucking awful shirt he was wearing. His dick chubbed up a bit at the thought of it, which Michael was frankly amazed at since his bollocks were about to drop off from the combination of cold and chafing.

He made his way along Queen Street to the Eldorado, went round the side, and banged on the door. It was answered by a woman around Michael's sisters' age, with short bleached-blonde hair in a messy bob and plenty of eye makeup. Rufus's big sis, maybe? Michael flashed her a smile on autopilot.

"Oh, hello," she said, smiling back.

Michael's smile broadened. Yeah, even soaking wet, wearing an old-man shirt, and flying on automatic, he was still fucking irresistible. Behind her, Michael could see an old bloke, grey-haired and in a saggy cardigan with leather patches on the elbows.

And Rufus, doing goldfish impersonations.

Fuck. What if he wasn't out to his family? Michael couldn't just leave him in the shit. Inspiration struck. "This is a B&B, right? I'm looking for a room."

"Oh," the woman said, not sounding too keen on the idea. "Um, well, sorry, but we're not actually taking bookings until Easter."

Michael wasn't having this. Especially as the chafing from his wet jeans was now so bad he'd probably end up with his thighs scarred for life. "Why not?"

She looked baffled for a mo, then rallied. "It's the Isle of Wight, see? Nobody comes here in February." She glanced back into the kitchen, maybe hoping someone would back her up.

Michael wasn't having *that* either. He pasted on his best smile, the one that always got the girls in the local chippie to give him extra crunchy bits for free. "Ah, but that's where you're wrong, innit? Cos here I am. You wouldn't wanna leave me wandering the streets of Sandown with nowhere to lay my head, now would you? And I'm sure you could do with a few extra quid—who can't? 'Specially a fashionista like yourself . . ." He let a gleam of admiration show in his eye as he raked his gaze over her ensemble of Topshop's finest. "I'll pay cash," he added.

No need to mention she'd have to dry the notes out with a hairdryer before she could bank 'em.

She giggled. "Well . . . What do you think, love?" She turned to the old bloke.

Bloody hell, he'd thought that was her *dad*.

The old guy looked uncertain. And not all that happy with the idea, which wasn't surprising. If Michael had known he was flirting with the much younger wife, he'd have dialled it *right* back. "I'm not sure . . ." He turned to Rufus.

What was this, a family game of pass the buck?

"No problem," Rufus said firmly. "Really not. I'll make up a room, and there's plenty of food for tonight. Why don't you come on in, Mi—I mean, whatever your name is, and I'll show you to your room?"

Thank God. "Cheers, mate," he said, stepping into the kitchen. "Appreciate it." He offered his hand to the old bloke—probably be a good idea to try to get him on side now. "Michael O'Grady. I'm from Southampton, just over here for a few days."

Yeah, he looked happier now. "Gerald Kewell. Lovely to have you to stay with us." He even managed to make it sound halfway sincere. "And this is my wife, Shelley"—emphasis on *my* and *wife*—"and my son, Rufus." Then he peered at Michael like he'd forgotten his specs. "You know, I've got a shirt just like that."

Rufus grabbed Michael by the elbow and steered him towards the stairs. "Right, come on, Michael, this way."

Once there was a safe distance between them and the folks, Michael turned to Rufus with a grin. "Now I'm a paying guest, shouldn't you be calling me 'Mr. O'Grady'?"

"We're very informal. Why are you here?" Rufus looked down at his feet. "I mean, not that I didn't want to see you again, and I know what they say about gift horses—"

"They got ribbons tied round their dicks? Wanna check mine out and see?"

"—but half an hour ago you were all, like, 'Laters, babe,' and now you're, well, back."

"Yeah . . . Fancied a change of hotel, that's all." Michael hoped Rufus wasn't gonna ask why he hadn't taken the time to get changed into dry clothes if that was the case.

"Oh. Ex-girlfriend? Yeah, I s'pose that must've been a bit awkward. Why'd you split up, anyway?" Rufus frowned. "Come to that, why were you in the sea? Was she really that bad you had to jump off the pier to get away from her?"

Michael thought fast. "Some things just ain't meant to be," he said mysteriously. Or gnomically, even, which had recently been on the word-of-the-day calendar his eldest sister, Faith, had given him for Christmas, so he knew it didn't mean "like a naff garden ornament."

Faith reckoned he had a vocabulary of around four hundred words, not including the rude ones, which was total bollocks. Michael knew what big words meant, right? Just cos he didn't go throwing them around all the time didn't mean shit. He'd even read a book, once.

"Right," Rufus said, opening a door into a bedroom that was large and light, with a big bay window that looked out the front. Nice. "This can be your room. I'll get sheets and stuff, but you probably want to get out of those wet clothes. Um, again." He blushed.

Michael gave him a slow smile. "Wanna help me? *Again.*"

"Uh, my parents are right downstairs . . ."

"And they don't know you're gay? Hey, no worries. I know what it's like. I'm not gonna grass you up." Michael started to undo his jeans.

Rufus paused before speaking. "Um, they know I'm gay. But . . . you just introduced yourself to them as a total stranger. Not as my boyfriend. Not that we're boyfriends," he added quickly, probably seeing Michael's *whoa* face. "Just, you know, the whole pretending we'd never met thing? Which I'm sort of wondering why you did?"

"Jesus, try to do a bloke a favour . . . So they're all right with you being a poof, then? The old man and the bit of fluff?" Michael pulled off his jeans and started inspecting his knackers to make sure they were still there and hadn't been worn down like worry beads.

"Well, yeah. I mean, they'd have to be, wouldn't they? It's not like anyone can do anything about it. Um. Do you want me to get you out some clean underwear?"

"Yeah, go for it," Michael said without looking up. "Should be a pair of jogging bottoms in there too."

There was the sound of his bag being upzipped. "Oh."

That didn't sound good. Michael glanced at Rufus, his tackle still in his hand. "What?"

Rufus was staring into Michael's bag with a weird expression on his face. "There's been a bit of, um, leakage. Shampoo, I think. And conditioner. And shower gel. Oh, and some toothpaste too." Now he mentioned it, Michael had wondered why the room suddenly smelled all herbal and spicy. With a hint of spearmint.

"Fucking hell." Michael shook his head, a grudging smile on his lips. You had to hand it to Trix: when she did vengeance, she didn't do it by halves. He was just glad she hadn't had access to a pair of scissors at the time. Or his bollocks, for that matter. "Shit. I'm gonna take a shower—bathroom down the hall, right? Just bung my kit in the machine for me, yeah?" The old-man shirt, now it was done up, would just about save him from indecent exposure if anyone came upstairs. Then he frowned at Rufus. "What's with the *Karate Kid* getup, anyway? And how come you're the one doing the room? What are you, Cinderfella or something?"

Still crouching down by Michael's bag, Rufus huffed. "Not all stepmothers are evil, you know. Looking after guests just isn't really Shelley's thing. And I'm wearing a bandana because *somebody* wrote on my head in permanent marker." He pushed up the scarf to show that, yeah, Michael's phone number was still there.

Michael cracked up. "See you later, Cinders."

CHAPTER 6
BOUNCE

Rufus's hands shook, just a little, as he got the clean sheets from the linen closet. He'd come back. Michael had come *back*. Why? What did it mean? Did it mean *anything*? He'd said he needed a room, which was fair enough, but it wasn't like the Eldorado was the only B&B in Sandown. It wasn't even the only B&B in Queen Street, and the Sunny Shores Lodge was closer to the high street *and* had its Vacancies sign out, because Mrs. Feltham-Brown thought a day spent not earning money was a day wasted.

So maybe, just maybe, Michael had wanted to see him again? Or was that just wishful thinking? After all, given the way he'd looked when Rufus had said the b-word . . .

No. No, that was defeatist. Rufus shook out the sheet with a snap, smoothed it down, and tucked it over the mattress. Then he started work on the duvet cover. Clearly it was just Poseidon looking after him. He'd caught Rufus's birthday present doing the walk of shame and had packed him straight back to the B&B.

Given that his firstborn wasn't on offer, Rufus wondered what sort of sacrifice Poseidon might accept instead to keep him feeling generous. He puffed up the pillows. Some kind of fish? All they had in the house right now were tins of tuna, which might not go down too well. And if anyone saw him chucking one in the sea, he'd probably get done for littering. But there had to be something Rufus could do to keep hold of Michael.

Just as Rufus gave the final tweak to the duvet, Michael swaggered back into the room, his damp chest hair plastered to him in intriguing swirls and his bits barely hidden by the hand towel clutched around his waist. "Forgot to give me a towel, dintcha? Gonna cost you stars on TripAdvisor, that is. Course, we could come to some arrangement about that." He let the towel fall.

Oh god. Rufus couldn't deal with this. Not with all the . . . feelings coursing queasily through him, and certainly not with Dad and Shelley in imminent danger of coming upstairs. Rufus picked up Michael's bag quickly. "I'll just get all this in the wash."

He grabbed Michael's wet jeans and Dad's shirt and hurried downstairs with them and Michael's bag. Shelley and Dad were sitting at the kitchen table, drinking tea.

Shelley stared at him. "Oh, love, he's not got you doing his laundry as well, has he? I hope you've told him we charge for that." She took another sip of tea.

Dad got up. "Let me do that. It's your birthday. You shouldn't be running around being a dogsbody for some stranger who just turned up at the door."

"No, no, it's fine. I've got it," Rufus insisted, keeping tight hold of Michael's bag. God knew what else might be lurking in its depths. Dad's innocence needed to be protected at all costs. "It'll be nice to have a bit of company anyway," he babbled on as he crouched down by the washing machine and threw in the jeans and shirt. "You know, liven up the long winter evenings . . ." He trailed off, flushing.

"Quite a looker, in't he?" Shelley put in idly. "Wonder what he's doing here, all on his lonesome?"

Dad frowned.

"I'll ask him," Rufus said quickly, pulling the rest of Michael's clothes from the bag and jamming them into the machine in one big bundle. He poured in detergent and switched it on.

"You don't have to cook for him tonight," Dad said, still frowning. "I'll explain we don't do dinners out of season. He can go out."

Rufus would have to find Michael something to wear first. "No, I don't mind. In fact, it'll be good to have someone new to cook for." It would, actually. Rufus never really felt their usual guests—or his family, for that matter—fully appreciated his cooking.

"I don't know," Shelley said doubtfully. "He doesn't look like a gourmet-dining sort of bloke to me. More a 'hunt it down, wrestle it into submission, and cook it on an open fire' sort of bloke. A real *man's* man." Her expression brightened.

Dad's frown deepened.

Rufus stifled the urge to shout, *Yes, he* is *a man's man, and* I'm *the man.* "I already told him he could stay for dinner. He's really looking forward to it," he lied.

"Oh, well, if you've told him already." Dad gave him a fond look. "I don't know what we'd do without you. Certainly wouldn't have been able to keep up the B&B after your mum got sick."

"Yeah," Shelley chipped in. "Best stepson a woman could have, you are."

Rufus never knew what to say when they went all sincere on him. "I'll go and see if Mic—I mean, Mr. O'Grady needs anything. Um. Is it all right if I lend him some stuff of yours, Dad? His bag had an accident."

"Oh—yes, of course. I don't suppose he'd fit into anything of yours, would he?"

"Not with them shoulders," Shelley said dreamily.

Dad was going to get permanent furrows from all this frowning. "Still, fortunately he and I seem to have similar taste in clothes. Yes, take anything you want."

Rufus escaped upstairs. He hadn't much liked the undercurrents down there. While he was of course absolutely certain Shelley wouldn't ever cheat on his dad, did she *have* to be so obvious about ogling another bloke?

Especially when he was *Rufus's* bloke. Well, sort of.

He rummaged through Dad's drawers and selected his items with care. Then he took them to Michael's room.

Michael was sprawled on top of the duvet, starkers. "Took you long enough, didn't it?"

"I brought you some clothes," Rufus said, trying not to stare. Except they'd already had sex, so why shouldn't he stare? He gazed defiantly at the muscular form laid out before him. Michael's skin, he decided, was as winter pale as Rufus's was—he just looked browner because of the thick, dark hair on his chest, arms, legs, and . . . other places. Oh god. Michael's dick was stiffening as Rufus looked at it.

Michael smirked. "Forget the clothes. Why don't you come here and warm me up yourself?"

"I can't! They're still downstairs. They might hear something."

"So?"

"So they'll think I'm a total slut! They think we've only just met, remember?"

Michael's smirk deepened. "Yeah, but when we screwed around before, we *had* only just met. *Remember?* Cos I fucking well do." He stroked his dick suggestively. "Bit late to come over all virginal on me now, sunshine."

"*They* don't know that," Rufus whispered furiously. "So put the clothes on, all right?"

Throwing them at him was possibly a bit excessive, but Rufus wanted them both to be absolutely certain he'd made his point. Facing his dad and stepmum after having his first experience of full-on sex with a stranger had been bad enough. He could *not* deal with them overhearing him having his second.

No matter how tempted he was to just jump into bed with Michael and let him have his wicked, wicked way with him again.

"Christ, you're no fun," Michael complained, sitting up and picking through the pile of garments that had landed on his chest. "Hang on a mo, what the fuck is this shit?"

"Dad's clothes," Rufus said, folding his arms. "The only ones that'll fit. So it's that or nothing, and if it's nothing, you'll go hungry, cos *I'm* not serving you dinner if you come down naked and give my dad a heart attack. Speaking of which, I need to get back in the kitchen."

"Why? You washing my kit by hand?"

Rufus didn't answer, too busy legging it downstairs before temptation got the better of him. This was all getting too much. What he needed was some quiet time alone in the kitchen prepping for tonight's dinner. That'd calm him down.

"That was quick," Dad said when he got back in the kitchen. They were still here? How long did it *take* to drink a cup of tea?

"So what did he say?" Shelley asked.

Rufus stared at her. "What?"

She *tutted* affectionately. "About why he's here on his own."

"Um, I forgot to ask," Rufus said. "I'll go and do it now."

He ran back upstairs, went into his room, and closed the door. Then he hid under the duvet.

CHAPTER 7
DROP

Michael gave his dick another couple of halfhearted strokes, but with Rufus no longer there, it'd lost interest. Shit. When he'd pictured what staying in Rufus's B&B would be like, he'd imagined a total shag-fest. He'd forgotten it belonged to his parents and they might actually *be* there a lot of the time.

Not that they'd have a leg to stand on, morals-wise, if they got uptight about him shagging their son under their roof. Again. Christ, how had the old goat pulled a girl young enough to be his daughter? She had to be thirty-five, forty tops, while *he* looked like he had both feet in the grave and a bloke standing by with a shovel. She had to be a gold digger. It was the only explanation, although fuck knew how much gold there was in a B&B on the Isle of bloody Wight.

He put on the old-man shirt Rufus had left him, then the old-man trousers which were too loose in the waist and too short in the leg. Rufus had brought him a pair of saggy white boxer shorts as well, but no way was he fucking touching those. Nylon socks— and Jesus Christ, a cardigan? Michael had to laugh. Sod it. If he was gonna look like a dork, he might as well go all the way. He pulled on the cardigan, and buttoned it up for good measure. Like the shirt, it was tight at the shoulders but sagged out at the stomach, giving him a phantom potbelly. Jesus wept. Michael jammed his hands in his pockets, let his shoulders slump, and looked in the full-length mirror in the wardrobe door.

Christ. If he went home like this, his mum'd have a heart attack, convinced his dad had faked his own death twenty-six years ago and had been living with some strumpet all this time.

Kind of weird, thinking what his dad might have been like if he'd lived. Michael had seen pictures, course he had, like the black-and-white one on the gravestone that'd creeped him out every Sunday when he was a kid and they went to visit it after Mass. It'd come from Mum and Dad's wedding photos, and to Michael his dad was always that dark figure in a black suit, looking a lot like the devil in one of his sisters' TV programmes. The pictures he'd seen of his dad playing with his sisters when they were little just hadn't seemed like the same man. More like some friendly uncle he'd never got to meet.

Michael shivered and turned away. Time to go see if Rufus's stepmum still fancied the pants off him when they belonged to her old man.

When he got downstairs, though, the kitchen was empty, the only sign of life his skivvies going round and round in the washer. A flash of crimson showed his sweater was in there as well, and Michael winced. His mum always washed it by hand.

What to do now? Michael wasn't gonna go outside dressed like some old grandad, that was for sure. He had a bit of a poke around. The cupboard under the stairs turned out to be a kiddies' games room, complete with an ancient portable telly and boxes of Lego. The door marked *Residents' Lounge* led to a big room with a bay window, which had to be directly under his bedroom. It had flowery curtains, comfy-looking mismatched armchairs, and a faint smell of furniture polish. No people, though, which Michael supposed he should have expected. There must be another living room somewhere, where the family went to get away from the guests.

Well, this was crap. Michael hadn't come here to be treated like a fucking customer.

He slouched moodily back to his room and took a look in his bag to see if there was anything salvageable. His phone dripped water when he picked it up, so he didn't dare turn it on. Better ask for some rice to bag it up with. Trix had not only emptied his toiletries bag of anything liquid, she'd refilled it for him. With shaving foam. His brand-new copy of *Bike* magazine had all the pages stuck together. Michael slung the lot back in the corner, his disgust mingled with grudging admiration for a job well done. Then an idea hit.

Hadn't checked out Rufus's rabbit hutch yet, had he?

After an automatic glance in the mirror—yep, he still looked like shite—Michael crossed the hallway to Rufus's door. Should he knock?

Nah. Michael opened the door and walked straight in.

For a moment, he thought the room was empty. Then he realised that what had seemed at first glance to be an unmade bed with the duvet left in a heap, was actually an occupied bed with someone *hiding* under the duvet. Michael grinned.

Then he leaped.

There was a muffled, "Argh!"

The lump in the duvet squirmed furiously, but was no match for Michael. Heh. He pinned it under his body, then peeled back the edge of the duvet until tousled blond hair and a bright-red face appeared.

"You wanker," Rufus said, gasping for air.

"Wank you off if you want," Michael offered, feeling in a giving mood. Then he remembered the clothes Rufus had brought him and felt a lot less generous. "Or you could give me that blowjob you owe me."

The pink forehead furrowed. It was kinda cute. "What do you mean, I 'owe' you?"

"Hey, we did what you wanted last time. This time it's my turn." Michael tried to grope Rufus's dick through the duvet, but it was pretty hard to tell what was what through fifteen togs' worth of hollowfibre.

Rufus's expression didn't magically change from annoyed to turned on, so he was fairly sure he'd missed and grabbed a knee or something. "There's not going to be a *this time*. My parents are still downstairs, you know. And the living room's directly under my room here."

"Yeah, but your dad's old. He's probably got the telly turned way up high."

Rufus pouted. Fuck, Michael wanted to bite that lip. "My dad's not old. He's just mature. And his ears work perfectly well, which is why we're not getting up to anything with them in the house. I need to do prep for tonight's dinner, anyway."

Michael sat back on his heels, still straddling Rufus. With the duvet in between them, it wasn't as much fun as it should have been. "Dinner? That's hours off."

"Yeah, but good food takes time." Rufus wriggled and pushed the duvet down off his arms and shoulders, leaving a bloody great wedge of it up against Michael's crotch.

Michael frowned. Something wasn't right here. "It's your birthday, right?"

"Yeah."

"So, leaving aside the whole question of why your dad and your evil stepmum have got you acting as their skivvy, why don't you just put your feet up and order a takeaway?"

Rufus stared at him. "Why?"

Michael stared back. It wasn't like he hadn't understood the question, cos it was only one word long and it wasn't even a *big* word. It was more like he instinctively knew Rufus wasn't gonna understand the answer. "Because cooking's boring as shite and it never tastes as good as what your mum makes, so why bother?"

Rufus blinked. "I like cooking. Always have."

"Why?"

"What's not to like? It's like making little artworks on a plate. And then you get to eat them at the end."

"Uh-huh." The closest Michael had ever got to art in the kitchen was when he'd put extra bits of ham on a pizza he was warming up for his tea cos Mum was ill, and made them form the shape of a penis.

It'd been a pretty impressive penis, mind. He'd added slices of salami for bollocks and extra cheese for spunk. Then he'd nearly wet himself when Mum came into the kitchen to check he hadn't starved to death just as he was taking it out of the oven. Luckily she'd been too woozy to notice anything, and he'd packed her straight off back to bed.

"I'm doing duck for tonight. Oh, and you're going to meet my best friend. Liz. She's a lesbian, but if you call her Lizzy the Lezzy she'll cut you." Rufus stretched his arms up and put them behind his head.

Great. Michael wasn't big on lesbians. They always seemed to hate him on sight, or at least as soon as he opened his mouth.

"She's bringing her baby round," Rufus added, rubbing salt in where he'd just stuck the knife.

Michael wasn't keen on babies, either. All they ever did, in his considerable experience as an uncle of seven, was cry, puke, and shit.

He'd liked all his nieces and nephews a hell of a lot better once they got out of nappies. Especially since his sisters had kept teasing him about making him change one cos he needed practice for when he was a dad. Didn't they realise it was making him wanna swear off women for life? Not that he would, obviously—Mum'd have a fit—but he certainly wasn't in any hurry to marry one.

"So if she's a lezzer, who's the dad? Some test tube somewhere and a turkey baster?"

"Nah, Liz was going out with this trans girl for a while and they got drunk one night and didn't use a condom."

Michael didn't ask. He didn't wanna know.

"She pays support," Rufus went on. "As much as she can. And she visits Kieran sometimes. But her girlfriend now is, like, dead jealous—I mean, seriously, she turns into the She-Hulk and starts smashing stuff—so it's sort of awkward."

"Who'd of thought it?" Michael said sardonically. Probably. *Sardonically* had been one of last week's words, and he wasn't sure he was remembering it right. "So tonight's dinner's gonna be you, your dad, your stepmum, and your best mate. And me, am I right? Look, no offence, but I reckon I'd be a lot more comfortable leaving you with all the happy family stuff and going out to the chippy."

Cos seriously, it was *way* too early for all the meet-the-family crap. Even if he *had* already met the family. And come to that, "never" would still be too early to meet the family, since this wasn't a relationship, was it? This was just a . . . a hookup. On a repeat setting. Hopefully. With added family. And friends. And talking to each other about stuff that wasn't just *there* and *harder* and *fuck yeah*.

Michael gave up trying to work out what this was. It was doing his head in. And anyway, Rufus was pouting again, and it was distracting him.

"I *want* you to come to my birthday dinner." His expression turned sly, or at least what passed for sly on Rufus's angel-perfect face.

Shit, Michael had it bad.

"It's included in the room rate," Rufus finished.

At least he wasn't so far gone not to catch an obvious lie. "No, it's not. *Bed and Breakfast*, yeah? That's what it says on the sign." Michael folded his arms.

Bad move. Rufus took his chance to wriggle out from under him and jump off the bed. "Yeah, well, it also says *Closed until Easter*, so suck it up and deal. You want a room here off season? You're coming to dinner."

CHAPTER 8
ESCALATE

Rufus ran down the stairs, wondering if he was playing a bit too hard to get. Especially since he'd been got pretty thoroughly once already today. After all, it was his birthday. And he wasn't a kid. Even if Dad and Shelley walked in on him with his ankles in the air and Michael's dick in his arse, they probably wouldn't get mad. Dad would just cough and mutter something about putting the kettle on, and Shelley would giggle and give him a nudge and a wink later. Probably.

On the other hand, it was kind of fun winding Michael up. And he really wasn't all that attractive in Dad's clothes.

Okay, that was a lie. He was still hot as hell. It just felt all sorts of weird and wrong getting turned on by him when he was dressed like that. Rufus was probably going to have sexual hang-ups for life because of it.

But he *did* need to get on with prep for tonight. And get Michael's clothes out of the washer and bung them in the dryer so Liz wouldn't laugh her head off at him when she came round tonight. He hoped she'd like Michael. Yes, yes, of course she would. What was not to like?

Rufus decided not to think about that question too closely.

He'd got downstairs not a minute too soon, anyhow, as Shelley was at the washer, sorting through Michael's things. "Ooh, don't he wear tiny little briefs?" she said, holding a bright-red pair up so Rufus could see. "You'd think he'd get pins and needles in his— Oh, hello, love." She smiled at Dad, who'd walked in at that moment and was now backing out again. "I was just helping Rufus with the laundry."

"That's all right, I'll take over now," Rufus said, before she could put Michael's sweater in the dryer and shrink it to Rufus's size. Although on the other hand . . . No, no, that wouldn't be fair on Michael.

"You're a treasure, love," Shelley said, sitting down at the kitchen table with a grateful *oof* and opening her magazine.

Rufus bunged the cottons in the dryer and hung the rest on the airer, by which time Michael had joined them. "Put the kettle on, would you, love?" Shelley asked without lifting her eyes from the latest celebrity scandal.

"Uh, right. Okay," Michael said, looking around the kitchen.

"Oh my God! Sorry, Mr. O'Grady, I thought you were Gerald." Shelley giggled. "It's the clothes. Mind you, they look a bit different on you."

She wasn't wrong. Oh god, had Rufus made a serious tactical error? Would seeing Michael in Dad's clothes just make her compare them all the more? And find Dad wanting? Worse, leave *Shelley* wanting?

"Call me Michael." He grinned. "Seeing as I'm wearing your old man's trousers and all."

"Michael, then. So what brings you to the Isle of Wight?"

Michael looked shifty. "Just fancied a break. Any chance of a cup of coffee?"

"Course, love. Is that kettle on, Rufus? And you'll make the coffee, won't you, love? You know I'm rubbish at it."

"Yeah, course," Rufus said, getting out the cafetière. "You want a cup of tea, Shelley?"

"Please, love. Why don't you come and sit down, Michael?"

Michael glanced at Rufus. "Uh, that's okay. I'll make the tea, yeah?"

"No, don't be silly. You're a guest." Shelley beamed at him and patted the chair next to her. "Now, if you want to read a newspaper, there's the *Mail* or the *Telegraph*, 'cept I'll have to get the *Telegraph* off Gerald. We normally get extra in during the season, but—"

"Uh, the *Mail*'s fine," Michael said. "Sure you don't wanna hand there, mate?"

Rufus stared at him, surprised. "No, thanks, I'm fine."

Shelley beamed. "In't he a treasure?"

The rest of the afternoon was a bit weird, with Michael hanging out in the kitchen while Rufus prepped the food and started cooking. Wasn't he bored? Nobody could take *that* long to read the *Daily Mail*. Especially as Michael only seemed to bother with the sports pages and the comic strips.

Liz turned up early for dinner, as usual, so she could offload Kieran onto Shelley and help Rufus in the kitchen. There was always stuff that couldn't be done in advance, so it meant he had some company while he was getting things finished off. Liz had done the same hospitality and catering evening class Rufus had, so she knew how to plate up a meal. Unlike, say, Dad or Shelley, neither of whom could be trusted to drizzle properly.

Like any good mate, Liz walked straight in the side door without knocking, a rucksack on her back and a toddler on her hip. Rufus was just straining the sauce, with Michael by his side making helpful comments like "I've never seen my mum do that" and "Why don't you just let us bung on some ketchup?" He'd changed back into his own clothes, which made him even more of a distraction. Fresh out of the dryer, Michael's jeans and T-shirt clung to him like a drowning man who'd decided he was going to get some before he died.

Rufus knew just what that felt like. He was sinking fast in a sea of hopeless need. What was worse, he didn't just want to shag Michael. He wanted to *hold* him afterwards. And before. And during. Which, based on past experience, would be received about as well as, say, a leftover limpet from Michael's dip in Sandown Bay.

Liz was rocking a Western shirt today, with a shoelace tie and a black suit jacket on top. Her light-brown hair was freshly shaved on the sides and gelled straight up on top, bringing her height almost to Rufus's shoulder level. Rufus had always thought she looked, from the neck up, a lot like the eggshell with a face drawn on he'd grown cress in when he was in primary school. Of course, he'd never dream of actually *telling* her so. Although once, in one of his bitchier moments, he had tried to persuade her to dye her hair green in honour of St. Patrick's Day so as to make the resemblance complete.

"Happy birthday, sausage jockey. Oi, what do you call a gay dinosaur?" Liz grinned. "Mega-sore-arse."

Rufus beamed at her. "All right, todger dodger? What did the first lesbian vampire say to the second lesbian vampire?" He paused for dramatic effect. "See you next month."

"Hey, I got one," Michael butted in. "What's the difference between a lesbian and a bowling ball?"

They both turned to glare at him, Rufus hoping he'd get the hint this was a private in-joke, not a dyke-bashing free-for-all.

Huh. Michael, get a hint? Maybe if Rufus had whacked him over the head with a sledgehammer with *HINT* embossed in the head, while a squad of naked cheerleaders with strategically placed pom-poms danced around shouting *H-I-N-T*. "You can only get three fingers in a bowling ball," Michael finished, and grinned expectantly.

Embarrassed, Rufus turned his back on Michael just as Liz did, in an unplanned display of synchronised shunning. "Who's that?" Liz hissed in Rufus's ear.

"Michael," he whispered back. "He's staying with us. Um. Also, we shagged."

She laughed. "Yeah, right. So go on, who is he?"

"I *told* you. I found him on Sandown beach earlier today, and he was all wet so I brought him home. And we shagged. And then he left, but he came back, so now Dad and Shelley think he's just an ordinary guest."

Michael's voice broke in. "I can hear you, you know. And oi, you said she was bringing a baby. This sprog's gotta be what, two and half? Three?"

"Twenty-seven months," Liz said proudly. "But he's big for his age, ain't you, little man? Already potty-trained, and he knows loads of words."

Kieran hid his curly head in his mum's shoulder.

"Yeah?" Michael smirked. "I know a few and all. Want me to teach you?" Okay, it was less of a smirk and more of a leer.

Liz's lip curled, and Rufus cringed just a little bit.

"*There* you are." Shelley's voice cut through the tense silence like a hot knife through Sachertorte. "Come and give your Auntie Shelley a cuddle, honey bun." Kieran looked round and started struggling, and when Liz put him down, he toddled into Auntie Shelley's arms with squeals of delight only slightly louder than Shelley's.

Rufus's heart clenched. He hoped she wasn't going to cry after they'd left, like she had last time.

"Michael," Shelley asked, "why don't you come and sit down with me and Kieran, and leave the experts to get on with it?"

"Uh, yeah. Sure." Michael turned to Kieran. "Come on, squirt, I'll race you."

Rufus didn't get to watch him pretending to run at toddler speed, cos Liz grabbed his arm and wrenched him round to face her. "You shagged *that*?"

"What, you think I can't pull someone that good-looking?"

"No, but I thought you had standards. Lemme guess, he's the sort who reckons there's no such thing as a lesbian, only a woman who hasn't been lucky enough to get up close and personal with his awesome ten-foot penis? And what do you mean, you found him on the beach? Someone throw him off the ferry?"

"Potatoes are burning," Rufus lied, and dashed back to the cooker.

Liz followed him. Bugger. "What do you mean, *shagged*, anyhow? You blew him, he blew you, anyone get their kit off, what?"

"The full monty," Rufus said smugly. "Both of us totally naked, in my bed, his dick in my arse. Orgasms *everywhere*."

"Aw, bless. Little Roo's all grown up now."

Rufus rolled his eyes. "Thanks, *Kanga*."

Liz ignored him. "So are you going out with him, or was it just a one-time thing?"

"Um. We should start plating up now."

Liz gave him a look, but as it was actually true this time, she just started serving out.

When Rufus went into the dining room with the first of the plates, he found Michael on all fours, being a horsey with Kieran on his back.

"What?" he said defensively at Rufus's wide-eyed look. "I got nephews and nieces."

"Ooh, how many?" Shelley asked as he turfed a giggling Kieran off and stood up, arms folded, back in full-on macho mode.

Rufus gazed at him adoringly at this glimpse of the sweet, creamy ganache beneath that hard, bitter chocolate shell.

"Uh, seven, at the mo. Faith and Hope have got three each. Charity's just got the one right now, but a set of twins on the way."

"Faith, Hope, and Charity?" Shelley asked. "Are they triplets?"

"Nah, but they're only a year apart. Well, you know. Two years altogether."

"Christ, your poor mum," Liz said, setting a couple more dinners on the table. "And then she had you."

She didn't actually *say* that must have been like adding insult to injury, but the implication was definitely there if you knew where to look.

"Yeah, but she had to wait ten years for me to come along—first boy in the family." Michael pulled out a chair and sat down at the corner of the table nearest the door, a smug expression on his face as if that Y chromosome had been all his own work.

"Aw, I bet you got spoilt rotten," Shelley was saying as Rufus headed back to the kitchen for the last couple of plates, only to find Liz had got there already.

"What would everyone like to drink?" Dad asked as Rufus sat down next to him, opposite Michael.

"Have you got any *cherry pop*?" Liz asked not very innocently, sitting between Michael and Kieran's booster seat.

Rufus kicked her under the table. At least, he thought he had, but Michael was now glaring at him with a *what the bloody hell was that for?* expression on his face.

"I don't think so, I'm afraid," Dad said, oblivious. "But there might be some lemonade."

"Never mind. I'll have a glass of the Pinot, please. But only one, cos I'm driving." Liz turned to Michael. "So, you been to the island before? Or is it all *virgin territory* for you?"

Rufus gave her a hard stare.

Michael looked puzzled. "Nah, I'm only in Southampton. We used to come here for holidays when I was a kid." He took a forkful of duck, while Rufus watched anxiously. Michael's reaction didn't disappoint. "Bloody hell, this is *amazing*. Where'd you learn to cook like this?"

Rufus beamed. "Books, mostly, and the telly. And a catering course. That's where I met Liz."

"He's so clever, in't he?" Shelley gave him a fond smile. "I can't even boil an egg."

"Funny choice for a winter holiday." Liz carried on with the interrogation, which Rufus was a bit miffed at. He'd been hoping to bask in the praise a little longer.

"Nah, it was my g—I mean, it was just a spur of the moment thing."

"What do you do for a living?" Dad asked.

Rufus had been wondering that.

"Service engineer. You know—if your washer or your dryer breaks down, I'm the bloke who comes to fix it."

Liz snorted. "Might have known it'd be something traditionally male."

Michael narrowed his eyes at her. "What do you do, then? PE teacher? Cop?"

"Full-time mum at the mo, actually. But I want to get into the hotel business, if I can manage to find childcare I can afford without selling both kidneys. Oh, sorry, is that not stereotypical enough for you?"

Dad coughed. "More wine, Michael?"

"Cheers." He ate another forkful of food. "Oi, Rufus, what's your career plan? You gotta be training as a chef because seriously, this shi—*food*'s awesome. My middle sis, Hope, yeah, she goes on all these gourmet cooking evening classes, but she's never cooked me anything half this good. So what, are you gonna go off and be the next Marco Pierre Whatsisface?"

Well, they said to be careful what you wished for. Rufus glanced at Dad and Shelley. "Too busy with the B&B."

Michael frowned. "Yeah, but—"

"I'd like to propose a toast," Dad said over him. "To Rufus. Happy fifth birthday, and many happy returns."

"Yeah, to Rufus," Shelley agreed, raising her glass. "Best stepson ever."

Rufus went pink with squirmy pleasure. "Um. Can I make one too? To Dad and Shelley, for being really great, and to Mum. Wish she could be here too. Um. No offence, Shelley." He took a big gulp of Pinot and stared down at his plate.

Dad put his arm around Rufus and gave him a hug. Then he coughed and did the Pinot-drinking-and-plate-staring thing himself.

"Right, well, I got a toast too," Michael said into the awkwardly emotional silence. "No, two toasts. First, here's to the best meal I ever had, and second, here's to my mum never finding out I said that."

Rufus beamed at him.

Yes. Definitely his best birthday since Mum had died.

Technically his *only* birthday, but still.

"We'll clear up," Liz said after they'd all finished. "I bet Kieran would like Auntie Shelley to read him a story."

"Are you sure, love?" Shelley asked.

Liz nodded. "Yep. We'll be fine. Michael's gonna help," she added slyly.

"Oh, but he's a guest . . ."

Liz smiled sweetly, ignoring Michael's furious *oi, wait a minute* look. "He insisted."

Shelley looked pleased. "Ah, bless. You're a treasure. Your mum must be so proud of you."

Michael smiled at her. He saved the glare for Liz and Rufus when they got back in the kitchen with the dirty dishes. Which Rufus thought was a bit unfair. *He* hadn't been the one to make Michael help out.

"So your mum and dad. Do they ever do *anything* around here?" he asked, grabbing a tea towel, presumably as a statement that *he* wasn't gonna be the one getting his hands wet washing the dishes.

Although fair dues, he *had* had them in water once already today.

"Yes," Rufus said defensively, getting going on loading the dishwasher while Liz collected pans from the stove. "I don't like anyone but me to clean my equipment, though."

Michael leered. "You can clean my equipment any time."

Liz made gagging noises. Michael turned to her. "You're just jealous. How'd it work, anyway, with you and the sprog's dad?"

Liz gave him an unimpressed look. "Well, when two people love each other very much . . ."

"Nah, I mean, I don't get it." Michael's face was screwed up like he was trying really hard to understand.

Bless. Rufus felt all warm and fuzzy towards him.

"You're a dyke cos you don't like dick, right? But then you go and shag a chick with a dick."

Okay, now Rufus felt slightly cooler and as if he'd been forcibly defuzzed.

Liz got right up in Michael's face, her eyes narrowed to little slits like a snake's. "I've got no problem with dicks. Well, not *actual* dicks, anyway. It's the man on the other end I've got a problem with."

"Why?"

"Jesus, do I have to spell it out? *Lesbian.*"

"Yeah, but . . . Girls are great, yeah, don't get me wrong. But blokes are too. And if it's not the actual tackle you're objecting to, what is it?" He whirled to face Rufus. "Come to that, what you got against tits?"

Rufus hesitated, put on the spot. "Um, they wobble?"

"Mine don't," Liz snapped.

Michael frowned. "That's the best bit. Well, that, or when you grab a handful and squeeze." He made gropey-hand gestures.

Rufus stared at him, fascinated and, strangely, a little bit turned on. Probably because he was remembering those hands grabbing onto bits of *him* and squeezing . . . Yep, definitely turned on now. He adjusted his jeans, which had become somewhat uncomfortable in the crotch area.

"Argh!" Liz threw down her dishcloth in disgust. "That's it. If you two are gonna hump each other in the kitchen, I'm out of here."

She stomped out in the direction of the living room, leaving Rufus and Michael alone.

CHAPTER 9
GAMBOL

Baffled, Michael watched her storm out. *Women.* "Christ, what's her problem? I was only trying to have a conversation. No one's humping anyone. I'm not even *near* you." He turned to Rufus, and noticed for the first time what was happening in his kecks.

Rufus blushed and held a saucepan in front of his groin.

Michael gave a slow, appreciative smile. "Then again, seeing as we're alone now, what's stopping us? Bet I could make you come in your pans."

Rufus's Adam's apple bobbed. "I'm pretty sure that's against hygiene regulations," he said shakily. "And you know how I wasn't happy about us doing anything upstairs while my parents are downstairs? Really not any happier with them in the next room. With my best mate. And her *child.*"

Michael stepped forward, eyes on the prize. "Like Liz is gonna let the kid come toddling in here. C'mon. One little hump." He grabbed the saucepan from Rufus's unresisting fingers and chucked it in the sink, hoping there was nothing breakable in there already. "You won't even have to get your kit off."

He grabbed a couple of handfuls of Rufus's arse and pulled him close. *Oh* yeah. Their dicks met through layers of denim, and were *very* happy to say hi to each other again. Rufus's mouth, his lips plump and slightly parted, was so fucking perfect it would've been a crime not to kiss it, and Michael was feeling particularly law-abiding this evening.

Rufus moaned as their lips met. Michael was nearly blown away. Forget what he'd said about Rufus's food being the best thing he'd ever tasted—the man himself deserved a whole fucking galaxy of Michelin stars. He deepened the kiss, letting his tongue rove Rufus's mouth. Fuck, yeah. All he needed to do now was unzip—

There was a cough. "I, ah, came to see if I could lend a hand," Gerald's voice said politely enough, but with a hint of steel.

Michael had no idea how he did it, but suddenly Rufus, instead of being nicely squished between him and the kitchen counter, was three feet away. "Dad!" he yelped. "Um. I can explain?"

Michael was glad *he* could. He braced himself for a parental explosion. Christ, *another* place was gonna kick him out on his ear. At least he'd got a good meal out of it. And all his clothes washed. Actually, come to think of it, he wasn't doing too badly, especially as they probably wouldn't remember to ask him for any money.

Gerald just smiled faintly. Weird. "No need for that," he said. "But I think perhaps I'll stay and dry up?"

Huh. They really *were* okay with Rufus being a poof.

Shit. Now Michael felt like he oughtta say something. "Um, sorry about . . ." He trailed off, not sure how to end that sentence. Corrupting Gerald's only child? He was still hoping the bloke didn't know about *that*.

"Not to worry," Gerald said. "How long did you say you'd be staying?"

"Um, until Saturday?" That was what he'd planned with Trix. And yeah, maybe he'd been thinking before about going home early and surprising his mum, but he'd changed his mind, all right?

"And what are your plans while you're here?"

"*Dad*," Rufus interrupted, still looking red-faced and as jumpy as Charity's rescue cat, which had once leapt three feet in the air when Michael had petted it without warning. "You can't interrogate him like that."

Gerald raised an eyebrow. "Can't I? He's staying in my house. I think I've got a perfect right to find out what his intentions are." His tone was still mild, but Michael did *not* like the look in his eye.

"*DAD*! You can't say that, all right? Nothing about intentions! You sound like some Victorian father trying to protect his daughter's virtue."

"Uh, 's all right," Michael muttered, feeling guilty. "Haven't really got any plans. Just thought I'd see the sights, you know?" An idea hit him, and he turned to Gerald. "Maybe Rufus could show me around, yeah? Not like you're busy here, is it?"

Gerald gazed at him for a mo, somehow coming over a lot more threatening than an old bloke in a saggy cardi had any right to do. "I don't see why not," he said, managing to imply that if he ever *did* see why not, Michael would be booted out of there so hard he wouldn't need a ferry to get back to Southampton.

Yep, that guilty conscience was really starting to bite now.

They didn't get another moment alone all evening. Michael had to admire the old bastard's persistence, even as he wondered how long Rufus was gonna have to wait before his dad let him get up to anything in the house. Till he was twenty-five? Thirty? Over his dad's dead body?

Heh. Kinky.

Or was it just *Michael* he didn't want getting frisky with any of his family members? Shit. Michael *knew* he should've dialled back the flirting with Shelley. Maybe Liz had said something to him? Like *Rufus and Michael are about to break all kinds of hygiene regulations in the kitchen.* Huh. If only.

Michael wondered how he could get back in the old bloke's good books. Then he wondered why he cared. It wasn't like he was gonna ask for Gerald's blessing on him and Rufus getting married, was it? Still, if Rufus knew his old man was happy about them being together, Michael might actually stand a chance of getting some before his dick dropped off due to lack of use.

He spent the evening in the family living room with them, watching one of Rufus's favourite comedy DVDs. It was all right, actually, especially after Lizzy the Lezzy left early on to get the sprog into bed.

He'd rather have had Rufus to himself. But there was still tonight . . .

Half an hour after they'd all turned in—he'd been planning to wait the full hour, but his dick got so hard just thinking about Rufus, he was worried his kecks were gonna rip—Michael climbed out of bed, padded to the door, and listened. Nothing.

Result. Now, should he chuck a shirt on? Trousers?

Nah, he was still in his skivvies. That'd do.

He pushed down the handle—slowly, slowly—and opened the door a crack.

Still no sounds of life. Thank fuck. He stepped onto the landing, wishing it was as bright there as in his room, where the street lamp shone through the curtains. Here it was so bloody dark, he was seriously afraid he'd get turned around and end up jumping into bed with Rufus's mum and dad.

He felt his way towards Rufus's door—and then the worst pain he'd ever felt stabbed him in the foot. He stumbled, and it got the *other* foot. *Jesus.* What the fuck *was* that? Michael slammed against the wall, failed to keep his balance, and toppled onto the floor with a curse and a *thud* that probably set off earthquake monitors in California. *Fuck*, that hurt.

A light went on, and Shelley's face appeared around the edge of her bedroom door. "You all right, love?"

Gerald's face joined hers.

Great, now both of them were staring at him sprawled on his arse in his undies. Michael supposed it was some consolation that at least his stiffy had died way down.

"Oh dear," Gerald said. "I'm afraid I dropped a box of Lego when I came up to bed. I was clearing out the games room, you see. Did I miss some?"

In the light spilling from their door, Michael could see, now, that the landing carpet—and in particular, the area around Rufus's door— was strewn with enough little primary-coloured plastic bricks to keep his nieces and nephews fighting over them for a week.

Michael narrowed his eyes. "You dropped 'em, yeah? Funny that. I didn't hear a thing." He knew his Lego. Even just tipping the stuff out gently made enough noise to wake the dead.

Gerald smiled. "Yes, you do seem to sleep very soundly. I'd have warned you about it, otherwise."

Michael's *arse* he would've. Which, by the way, wasn't too impressed with the Lego bricks he was still sitting on.

Michael got gingerly to his feet. He half thought of just flipping them the finger and carrying on down the hall to Rufus's room, but somehow he wasn't feeling in the mood anymore. Rufus would probably just tell him to piss off anyhow.

He limped painfully back to his room, to the sound of Gerald and Shelley wishing him a good night.

Yeah, right.

CHAPTER 10
SKIP

Michael didn't seem to be in a very good mood when he came down to breakfast the next morning. Maybe he hadn't slept well? Rufus had slept *brilliantly*, once he'd taken care of a little problem that came up every time he thought about Michael, in bed, less than twenty feet away. Oops. Better stop thinking about him right now, in fact.

"Good morning," he sang out, cracking eggs into the frying pan. "Sunny-side up?"

Michael glowered at him from beneath the tousled mane of his hair and the sleek, hairy caterpillars of his eyebrows. "Fuck off and die."

Aw, bless. "There's coffee in the pot, or I'll make some fresh tea if you'd rather have that."

"Jesus, who are you? Mary fucking Poppins?"

Rufus stopped flicking oil over the yolks and put his hands on his hips. "No, but I'll send you to tidy your room if you don't clean up your language a bit, Mr. Clearly Not a Morning Person. My dad and Shelley are only in the other room."

"Yeah, well, they deserve all they get. You know your dad booby-trapped the hallway last night, don't you? I've got bruises on my fucking feet."

Rufus stared. "What did he do?"

"Are you seriously telling me you slept through all that? Put out Lego like fucking—what do they call 'em? Those things ninjas chuck on the floor to cut your feet up."

"Uh, caltrops?"

"That's the ones. Hurt like fuck. Seriously, what's your dad's deal? You're twenty years old. An adult. What's he wanna do, keep you locked in a tower like a short-haired Rapunzel?" Michael caught Rufus's expression and dropped his gaze. "What? My nieces like Disney films, all right?"

"That's sweet," Rufus said reassuringly, because it was. "Wait, you tried to get to my room last night?" If there had been one little lump in the béchamel sauce of his happiness, it had been the nagging fear that Michael might have lost interest in him. He beamed.

"Yeah," Michael grumbled. "Didn't get far, though."

Rufus slid the eggs onto the toast that had been keeping warm at the bottom of the grill, garnished each plate with crispy bacon, sausage, tomatoes, mushrooms, and a slice of black pudding, because even though no one ever ate it, it was *traditional*, and sat down at the kitchen table next to Michael. "Tuck in."

He watched with approval as Michael went first for the perfectly done egg yolk, which broke and spilled bright-yellow sunshine over the white. Then he snatched the bottle of brown sauce away before Michael could pollute his culinary excellence. "Taste the *food*, not industrial-strength vinegar."

Michael griped, but shoved a bit of egg-yolky toast in his mouth unsullied. "Happy?" he mumbled through his mouthful. Then his expression changed, and he chewed more thoughtfully.

"See?" Rufus said smugly. "That's the difference between supermarket tat and really fresh eggs from happy hens. I get them from a little farm near Arreton. *Anyway*, Dad's just worried about me. Well, about you, really. Not being local, and being older and all that. How old are you?"

Michael swallowed. "Twenty-six, and last I heard I've got a good few years to go before I get to dirty old man, ta very much. And like *he's* got a leg to stand on, for Christ's sake." He grabbed for the coffee.

"No, um. It's not the age difference, exactly. It's more, um . . ." Rufus bit his lip, laughter bubbling up, and lowered his voice. "I got the whole talk last night after you went to bed. He's worried you might want, um, *more than I'm ready to give.*" He gave Michael a significant look.

Michael stared at him for a moment. Then they both burst out laughing.

"Christ," Michael said after he'd calmed down a bit. "What does *he* think you're ready for? Holding hands? Or is that a bit racy for him?"

"Well, sexting is going to be out, obviously, but I think he might let us exchange letters. As long as he gets to censor any unsuitable content."

"Christ. How do you live like this?" Michael was rapidly getting through the bacon on his plate. Rufus felt a dangerous urge to give him some of his own, which had to be resisted at all costs. His heart, yes. Prime rashers of organically reared bacon from the island's best pig farm, no.

"Well, it helps living in a place with a really small dating pool. Have you got a place of your own?" He couldn't keep the wistful tone out of his voice.

Michael paused, a bit of black pudding on his fork. "Nah. Live with my mum." He popped the forkful into his mouth and ate it with every appearance of enjoyment. Rufus was impressed.

"What's *she* like when you bring boys home?" Rufus thought about it. "Or girls, obviously."

Michael hesitated again before he answered. "Mum's okay with it. Sort of." He laughed. "Sorts out the women from the girls, having 'em run the gauntlet of my mum in the morning."

"Oh god, what does she do?"

"Not a lot. Cooks 'em breakfast, usually. It's more the way she does it. That, and the comments about how *her* daughters never spent a night away from home before they were respectably married. Which is bollocks, as it happens, but don't let my mum know or my sisters'll skin me. There's an extension round the back of the house with a flat roof, and they used to climb out the window onto that and get out that way."

"What, and your mum never caught any of them?"

Michael put his fork down on his empty plate and rubbed the back of his neck. "Well, I always wondered if she knew and just pretended she didn't, but Charity swears she'd have hit the roof if she'd known."

"Pun not intended?"

"What?"

"Forget it. So have you ever brought anyone back you had to chuck out that way? Like, you rolled over in the morning and thought, 'Oh bloody hell, I can't introduce *this* one to my mum'?"

Michael laughed. "Gimme some credit. If they're not fit to meet Mum, they don't get past the front door."

"Must be a bit of a pain, though. I mean, sometimes you *want* to get together with someone the parents wouldn't approve of." Like Michael himself, say. Picking an example *entirely* out of the air. "Don't you ever think about moving out?"

"Nah, living at home's cheaper. And Mum does all the cooking and housework and stuff." Michael went a bit red, possibly at Rufus's disapproving look. "Hey, I give her money every month."

"That's very generous of you," Rufus said insincerely.

"Fuck off. She likes it, all right? Me being at home. It's company, innit? She doesn't wanna rattle around in that house all by herself. And she's *told* me that, before you say anything." Michael leaned back, his mug of coffee in his hands.

Was there a polite way to ask if someone was dead? Maybe Dad or Shelley would know, but Rufus was a bit stumped, and he couldn't exactly call them in and ask in front of Michael. Oh, sod it. "What about your dad?"

Michael shrugged. "Died before I was born."

"Oh my god, I'm so sorry." Rufus couldn't imagine that. It'd been bad enough losing Mum in his teens—but at least he'd known her. Had memories of her. Michael had never even *met* his dad.

Who'd done all the dad stuff with Michael, like playing cricket on the beach and pathetically failing to get kites to launch on the cliffs? Who'd given him lifts to school discos, and lectured him when he was ten minutes late back from the firework display cos he'd been snogging Andrew Harding under the pier?

And, all right, *technically* mums could do that sort of stuff too—Liz would gut him if he ever suggested she couldn't do that for Kieran, and he supposed even straight mums could probably make a fair stab at it—but it seemed a bit harsh Michael's mum had had to do the dad stuff as well as all the cuddling, temperature-taking, label-sewing, and sticking on of plasters. Poor Michael, getting only fifty percent of the love.

Was it easier, Rufus wondered, or harder, having only one parent to worry about not loving you anymore when you came out as gay? Both Mum and Dad had been brilliant about it, but that didn't mean Rufus hadn't *worried*. But at least, with two, you could hope one would still love you and get to work on talking the other one round.

"Did she never get married again?" he asked, trying to get his head round it.

"Nah. Don't think she ever thought about it, even. She goes on about him all the time, even twenty-six years later. Charity reckons she's never got over him dying, but she seems all right to me."

"Was it sudden?"

"Just a bit. He was a brickie, yeah? He was working on the roof of a block of flats when his foot slipped. Ended up taking the quick way down." Michael huffed a laugh. "Must've scared the crap out of the rest of the crew when he came sailing past."

Rufus winced. "That's, like, so tragic."

"Course, Faith reckoned he'd been out on the piss the night before. Anyway," Michael went on, standing up. "You're taking me out somewhere today, right? Showing me the sights of the Isle of Wight. And for Christ's sake take that fucking scarf off your head before we go out."

"I *can't*, can I?" Rufus glared at him. "Marker on the forehead, remember? I had another scrub at it last night, but it's still not come off."

"Jesus. You want nail-polish remover for that. You never heard of that? Are all your mates boring or something?"

"We don't make a habit of drawing on each other's faces when passed-out drunk, if that's what you mean."

"Yeah. Boring."

"You know, I'm really not looking forward to meeting your mates."

Michael seemed startled by something for a mo. Then he shook it off. "Yeah. Whatever. So get yourself sorted and we're out of here, yeah?"

Twenty minutes and half a bottle of Shelley's nail polish remover later, they were sitting in Dad's car, driving through Sandown and out Shanklin way.

"I can't believe your dad let you borrow his car. Ain't he worried I'm gonna shag you on the back seat?" Michael looked round hopefully. Then his expression turned suspicious. "Or has he booby-trapped that and all?"

"Don't think so, but I'm not gonna risk it. There's not enough air freshener in the *world*." Rufus shuddered at the thought of the mildly disappointed looks Dad would give him. That was if he was in a good mood. If he was in a *bad* mood, it'd be fake-puzzled frowns and insistent requests that Rufus tell him what on earth that funny smell might be.

Michael huffed a laugh. "Yeah, and if we left any stains on the upholstery, he'd probably skin me to replace it."

"You know, you've got totally the wrong idea about my dad. He's all right, really."

"Yeah? Tell that to my feet. And my tackle. My balls think my dick's been cut off." Michael yawned and scratched himself. "Where are we going, anyway? Aren't we gonna run out of island if we go much further?"

"It's not that small. Twenty-five miles across at the widest bit. And we haven't even got to Ventnor yet." They were driving through Shanklin Old Village now, with its thatched cottages and Ye Olde Shoppes selling tourist tat. Well, in the summer they would be. Most of them were closed right now. Michael was staring out of the window, but Rufus couldn't tell if he liked what he saw or hated it.

"Ventnor's the place at the bottom, right?"

"Yeah." The Isle of Wight was shaped roughly like a diamond, with Ventnor more or less at its southern point, and Sandown up along the coast towards the eastern corner. "You been there?"

"Nope. Is it worth it?"

"It's got some good restaurants. And a beach. And a pub."

"Show me one place on this whole bloody island that *hasn't* got a beach and a pub."

"Well, Newport, for a start. That's right in the middle of the island, so there's no beach there. Although there's plenty of pubs. And it has got a harbour cos of the river. Anyway, we're not going to Ventnor. Or Newport. Although Newport's not bad, these days, for a night out. It's got a big cinema and a couple of decent places to eat. I keep hoping they'll get a gay bar. Dad remembers when they didn't even have any high street chain shops."

They were out of Shanklin now, and the view opened out over the bay as the road climbed. Rufus loved this view, which stretched back along the coast to white-faced Culver cliffs at the far end. It wasn't as good as driving over Brading Down, where you could see the bay on one side and the mainland on the other and you really *felt* like you were on an island, but it was close.

"So where *are* we going?" Michael asked again. He must have been a right pain on car trips when he was a kid, Rufus thought fondly.

Perfect timing, though. "Here." Rufus pulled into the car park of the Cliff Top Café and parked at one end.

Michael didn't look impressed. "Hate to break it to you, but this place is closed. Or closed down."

"They're just shut until the start of the season. Come on." Rufus got out of the car and stood there tapping his foot until Michael followed suit.

"This better be worth it," he grumbled.

Rufus grinned, his anticipation not the only thing that was rising. "It will be. This way."

CHAPTER 11
SOAR

Michael followed Rufus around the back of the café, with its sun-trap conservatory facing the sea, and down the sloping lawn. It'd be a great place to lie out in the sun come August, but right now you'd freeze your nadgers off.

There was a small, knackered-looking wooden construction at the bottom. It wasn't exactly a shed—more like a sort of posh bus shelter, Michael thought as they rounded the back of it. There was a long, wide bench inside, with walls on three sides and a view out to the front that showed why someone had bothered to put it here, closer to the shipping lanes than the bus routes.

Michael stepped up to the fence just beyond it. Reddish cliffs dropped away beneath him, sloping down to the sea, which cliffs weren't supposed to do in Michael's opinion—*proper* cliffs were white and went straight down, like the ones you could see from Sandown Pier, so if you fell off the top, the next stop was *splat* on the rocks at the bottom. The worst jumping off these ones might give you was a nasty graze, or maybe a scratch from the gorse bushes that dotted them. The sea, though—it looked about three miles deep and three thousand miles wide, with a rich blue-green colour and not a single sodding ship to be seen. It was like standing at the end of the world.

Rufus slung his arms around Michael's waist from behind and laughed in his ear. "I can't *believe* you're looking at the view."

"What am I s'posed to be doing, then?" Michael asked, narked.

"Me."

Michael went from *uh?* to *fuck, yeah* in nought point three seconds. He twisted around in Rufus's arms and gave him a hard kiss that left them both panting. Caution made him ask, before all the blood drained south and he didn't give a shit anymore, "You sure we're not gonna get caught?"

Rufus's grin was so fucking cheeky it should have been illegal. Christ, Michael loved that smile. "I never have before. Dad knows the people who own this place, and they always spend the winter in their house in Spain. Welcome to the Love Shack."

He pulled Michael back into the bus shelter. Which, huh, lived up to its name, cos the stiff (heh) breeze he'd felt out by the fence was blocked by the walls. It was almost cosy. Not that Michael gave a shit. He was too busy feeling Rufus up. "So how many blokes you brought here, then, you tart?" He nibbled at the soft skin on Rufus's neck, just below the line of barely there stubble. Jesus, that was tasty.

"Hundreds. Thousands." Rufus laughed, the vibrations in his throat catching at Michael's lips and going straight down to his balls. "Two or three. Or four, maybe. Possibly five—"

Michael shut him the fuck up with another kiss. He didn't wanna think about Rufus giving it up for anyone else. He gave Rufus's arse a squeeze before pulling back. "Gonna blow me, then?"

Rufus's lips were plump, wet, and curved up at the edges. Cocky little sod. "Depends. You gonna blow me?"

Which was a no, obviously, cos sucking dick was something gay boys did and Michael wasn't gay. "Maybe," he hedged. "You do me first."

Rufus's eyes narrowed. It was too fucking cute. "Why do I get the feeling I ought to get something in writing before I start?"

Michael laughed. "Cos you're not as stupid as you look?" Not that Rufus actually looked stupid. He looked like he oughtta be a bestseller for Twinks"R"Us.

Rufus grinned and gave him the finger. "Bastard." Then he pushed Michael down onto the bench, which wasn't the way things usually went—usually Michael was the one doing the pushing, but hey, whatever. "Come on, flop it out. I haven't got all day."

"Oi, it's not gonna fucking *flop*." Michael undid his jeans. His hard dick was already poking out of the top of his briefs, moisture leaking from the tip. He shoved the front of his kecks down roughly, unable to stop a groan. Jesus, he'd been waiting for this for so fucking *long*.

"Bet I can make it flop." Rufus dropped to his knees and plunged his mouth down over Michael's dick in what Michael would swear was one continuous movement. Well, if he could get the words out, cos fuck, that was *incredible*.

He'd always reckoned there was no such thing as a *bad* blowjob, but there was good and there was fucking awesome, and Rufus was fucking awesome at sucking dick. And Christ, what a view. Rufus's hair was all tousled, and his dark-blond eyelashes brushed cheeks with bones you could cut yourself on, especially when they hollowed as he sucked. And those lips . . . Jeez, those lips. Michael had no words. No fucking words.

Electricity was fizzing up Michael's spine and his balls were drawn up tight, ready to explode. He had that heavy feeling in his belly that meant it was all gonna kick off any minute.

"You're gonna swallow, right?" he gasped out.

Rufus nodded—well, Michael reckoned it was a nod, but seeing as his dick was still in Rufus's mouth, that was all it took for him to come so hard everything went black for a mo.

When Michael's vision came back, Rufus was licking the last bit of jizz off his lips. Which, fuck, should not have made Michael wanna kiss him, but it just *did*, all right? Michael pulled him up and onto his lap. "You're heavier than you look," he said, and kissed him hard.

Tasting his own spunk was never Michael's favourite thing, but it wasn't so bad on Rufus. Cos Rufus was *really* into kissing, yeah, which the guys Michael usually went with often weren't, and since Rufus was a bloke, Michael could let go, be as rough as he liked. Rufus gave back as good as he got, twining his fingers into Michael's hair and pulling with exactly the right amount of force.

Rufus moaned into the kiss, which was a fucking turn-on, and let go of Michael's hair to scrabble at his jeans like he was desperate, which was even better. He broke the kiss with a cute little whimper. "Shit. Gimme a mo, here."

Rufus opened up his jeans with shaky hands and freed his dick from his boxer briefs. Christ, that was a thing of beauty. Then he grabbed Michael's hand and wrapped it round the hot, hard shaft. "Just jerk me off. I know you don't wanna blow me."

Which, yeah, was true, but it felt . . . off having him come out and say it like that. Like Michael was being a shit about it. "I could blow you," he found himself saying.

"'S okay." Rufus's fingers settled over Michael's.

Jeez. Try to do a guy a favour. "I'm gonna blow you, all right?" Michael pushed Rufus off his lap. "Sit."

Rufus sat. Michael pushed his legs apart and knelt down between them.

At least the floor of the shelter was wood, not concrete. It was still fucking hard and cold on his knees. Michael eyed the stiff cock bobbing in front of his face. Shit. He was gonna do this.

Shit. Would that make him gay?

No, it was okay. Cocksucking only made you gay if people knew about it, right, and no one was gonna know. He leaned forward, grabbed hold of it, and opened his mouth to guide it in. Rufus's dick tasted . . . pretty much like he'd expected, actually. Salty, with a strong musky smell flooding his nose from Rufus's neatly trimmed pubes. It was okay.

Then he looked up and saw Rufus gazing down at him, his eyes wide like he couldn't believe what was happening, and suddenly it was fucking *fantastic*. Rufus's mouth was open and letting out little panting breaths, and Michael hadn't even *done* anything yet, just shoved his dick in his mouth.

He pulled back and ran his tongue over the head. Rufus gasped, so he did it again. Jesus, why did some girls make such a big deal over giving head? This was *easy*. Way simpler than trying to find a clitoris in a fucking haystack.

Michael really got into it after that, remembering all the things he liked done to him and having a go at doing them to Rufus. He couldn't suck on Rufus's balls or finger him further back, cos he still had his jeans on and the angle was all wrong, but he worked his way through the rest of the tricks he'd picked up.

Rufus was trying to say something, but Michael ignored him. Who the fuck talked during sex?

Then hot spunk spurted in his mouth.

Whoa. Michael jumped back and fell on his arse just as another jet hit him in the face.

Christ, that was fucking gross. He'd forgotten about that bit. "Jesus, you coulda warned me." Grimacing, Michael wiped off his face with the back of his hand and glared at Rufus, who was red-faced and panting and still fucking gorgeous.

"I did! What did you think 'Stop, I'm gonna come' meant?"

Oh. Fair enough. Michael levered himself to his feet and grinned down at Rufus. "So what do you reckon? Fucking awesome for a beginner, or what?"

Rufus grinned back. "Not bad for a first attempt. You've got, um, something in your eyebrow."

"Lick it off," Michael said, cos he thought Rufus actually might.

"Come here, then." Rufus zipped up his jeans and lay back along the bench. There was just about room for Michael to join him, so he did. Rufus snuggled in against him.

He wasn't a cuddler, Michael wasn't. But it was nice, all right? Rufus pressed tight up against him like he'd been moulded to fit, he was warm, and he smelt good. Michael couldn't see his face from this angle, but he liked to think of him lying there, smiling.

"I'm not licking your eyebrow," Rufus said after a mo.

"Wuss. Call yourself a gay boy?"

"Yeah, but I've got to draw the line somewhere." He reached up and wiped it off with his thumb, though, so Michael didn't mind too much.

Lying on the hard bench, a warm Rufus in his arms, Michael gazed around idly and realised the inside of the place was covered in graffiti. And not the usual *Gazza is a wanker* sort. Some was in pen, and some had been scratched in the wood, but almost all of it was initials and dates, the initials in pairs and connected by plus signs or the number four, and a lot of them inside hearts. "Fuck, this really is a love shack, innit?"

"Yeah. Been here, like, decades. See the dates? There's one from 1980, one from 1973 ... The earliest I've seen is 1967. Wasn't that the original Summer of Love?"

Fuck if Michael knew. Even his mum hadn't been old enough to get involved in *that*.

"And see that one?" Rufus pointed into one corner. "*AR and GK, 1977*. That's my mum and dad's initials—Alison Robins and Gerald

Kewell. They were childhood sweethearts, except they split up and then got back together again ten years later. I mean, I don't *know* it was them here, cos I've never asked, but it's nice to think it was, innit?"

Michael reckoned there was nothing that'd make his dick go limp faster than the thought of being somewhere his mum and dad had shagged, but horses for courses. Then he frowned at the date. "You're saying your dad was a kid in 1977?" That was the year Michael's mum and dad had got married. He remembered, cos she always went on about it being the Queen's Silver Jubilee that year and how the local pub had just kept the bunting up for a few extra weeks until they had their wedding reception there.

"He was eighteen. He's fifty-seven now. Why, how old did you think he was?"

Fifty-seven? That was Michael's mum's age. "Christ, I dunno. Seventy?" He couldn't believe Mum and Gerald were the same age.

"Ouch. Don't tell him that."

"Not my fault, is it? He should dye his hair or something. They grow up on the island, then, your mum and dad?"

"Yeah, then Mum left to go to uni. She was really clever—got a first in English, which is supposed to be, like, really hard."

No one in Michael's family had ever been to uni. He'd left school with a handful of iffy GCSEs and a muttered *"Good riddance"* from most of his teachers. He'd always worked better with his hands than with his brain. "You ever think of doing that?"

Rufus was silent for long enough that Michael lifted up on his elbow to look at him. "Difficult question, was it?"

Rufus sighed. "I don't want to do anything, like, academic, but I've always had this dream of training to be a chef. I mean a proper one in a Michelin-starred restaurant, not just your bog-standard hotel cook."

Michael frowned. "Why don't you, then? You're good enough." Not that he knew anything about it, but he had taste buds, didn't he? That meal last night had been fucking fantastic. Breakfast had been pretty bloody good too.

It was going to ruin him for Mum's cooking.

"Can't. Dad needs me in the B&B."

"What about your evil stepmum? Can't she pull her finger out and take over?"

"Shelley's not evil, all right? She's . . . just not very good at that sort of stuff."

"What, hard work?"

"Don't be a git. She's been really great for my dad. Cheered him up loads."

Michael sniggered. "I bet she has."

Rufus shivered and sat up. "We'd better get going."

"Why? There someone else waiting to use this place?"

"Nah, but we'd better go somewhere proper. You can bet Dad's gonna ask questions over dinner tonight."

"So we'll eat out. You cooked last night."

"Well . . ."

"Go on. Live a little."

"I'd have to let Dad know."

"Later." Michael got up, impatient now. "Come on, I wanna see some sights. Hey, are we anywhere near that place with the dinosaurs? I don't mean that museum in Sandown. I mean the big ones you can climb on."

Rufus grinned. "Bless. What are you, five? Sorry, but Blackgang Chine won't open until Easter."

"We could go in over the fence?" Michael suggested hopefully as they scrambled back up the sloping lawn to the car park.

"Yeah, great idea, if you want to be front-page news in the *County Post*. They do have security, you know. And the off-season's when they do all the work around the place—maintenance and stuff. There's probably loads of people there."

"Sod it. That was the best bit of holidays here."

Rufus slung an arm around Michael's shoulders. "I'm getting this really cute picture of you as a kid. Sort of like a cross between Christopher Robin and Tigger."

Michael shrugged. He could live with that. Christopher Robin was all right, at least when he wasn't dressed in a girlie smock like in the original books—Christ, what were his mum and dad *thinking*? And Tigger was the cool one who had all the fun.

"Where did you used to stay?" Rufus unlocked the car, and they climbed in.

"Dunno, really. Some holiday park on the coast. We used to stay in chalets, mostly, but I reckon there was a caravan once." Michael frowned as he struggled to remember at the same time as fiddling with his seat belt. "It was a long time ago. Once all my sisters got too old to wanna come, Mum didn't bother with holidays no more. S'pose I was seven or eight the last time."

"Must've been nice, though. Family holidays." Rufus pulled out of the car park and back onto the road.

"What, you never had any?" Jesus, his dad must be a right stingy git.

"We run a B&B, remember? And live in a tourist resort? It's not like there's loads of money in it for going abroad off-season and stuff, and I was always at school anyway. Mum and Dad went abroad lots of times before they had me, so I s'pose they felt they'd done it all already. Um." Rufus went quiet for a mo. "What are we doing here? Really? I mean, like, you and me?"

Michael shrugged, feeling suddenly put on the spot. He stared out the car window. The road had gone inland, and he couldn't see the sea anymore. "Having a bit of fun."

He felt bad as he said it, *wrong*, and it got worse as the silence went on. But that was all it *could* be, right?

Rufus spoke. "You don't wanna try, you know, going out together?"

"What, like boyfriends and stuff?" Michael found it hard to keep the sneer out of his voice as he said the word "boyfriends." It just crept in there, like on automatic. He didn't *do* relationships with guys, all right? Guys were for fucking around with. If he wanted someone to go out with, he found himself a girl. Someone he could take home to Mum—could take out anywhere and not care who saw them. "You know I'm only here until the end of the week, right?"

And that . . . that *didn't* make his gut twist with hurt and regret.

It was just . . . indigestion. Or something.

"Yes," Rufus said with a lot more enthusiasm than Michael would've expected. "That's why it's perfect. You can have, like, a trial run of me."

Michael's guts untwisted themselves cautiously, like a hedgehog peeking one eye out to see if the coast was clear. "Yeah? What happens at the end when I go home?"

"We can sort that out then. You know. Decide if it's worked, and, you know. Sort something out." Rufus's ears had gone pink.

This was a bad fucking idea. Michael knew that. But shit, it was tempting. *Could* something work out between them? After all, Rufus was fun to be with—at least, when his dad wasn't around—and all that enthusiasm when they shagged was a serious turn-on. Not to mention the way Rufus looked, which was like he really oughtta be a model. In a porno mag. Michael wouldn't ever be able to take Rufus home to his mum, obviously, but they could meet up places. Maybe he could persuade him to move off the island? That'd be perfect. Rufus could get a room somewhere and maybe do that chef's course he wanted.

And Michael could go round and see him there, where no one would know about it. Yeah. That'd work. That'd be fucking *brilliant.*

"It was just an idea," Rufus said in a small voice with hints of Brave Little Toaster. (Shut up. His nephew Sean fucking loved that film.) "Doesn't matter."

Shit, he'd been silent too long. "No." Michael said it quick, without thinking. "I mean, yeah, why not? We'll give it a go."

Rufus's smile made him glad he'd said it. It was like a fucking ray of sunshine on a cold March day—wide and happy and Christ, it made him wanna kiss that mouth.

"Any more love shacks around here?" he asked hopefully.

CHAPTER 12
SOMERSAULT

Walking back into the B&B that evening, Rufus felt all fizzy, like a bottle of Coke that'd been shaken up and left for some poor unsuspecting person to open unawares. No, not Coke. Like a magnum of champagne, right, just before the Grand Prix winner sprayed it all over the crowd. Michael was going to be his boyfriend. *Was* his boyfriend. And okay, he didn't live on the island, but Southampton was only a ferry ride away. Michael could come over all the time. Every weekend, or whenever he had his days off. For evening dates, even. The hydrofoil took, like, twenty minutes, and even the car ferry got there in an hour. It was just like getting a bus. Only wetter. And more expensive. Maybe they had season tickets?

Or Michael could move. There must be *loads* of washing machines on the Isle of Wight that needed repairing, what with all the hotels washing sheets and towels every day. And it wouldn't be like he was leaving his mum on her own, cos, see, only a ferry ride away. She could come and visit as often as she wanted. Or she could move too. Lots of old people moved to the island when they retired. Rufus was sure she'd like it here. And he was sure he'd like her. He liked Michael, after all.

Michael's mum would like him, he knew it. Most people seemed to like Rufus, especially people's mums. He wasn't sure exactly why, but he wasn't going to complain, either.

And Michael liked him. He really, really liked him.

They'd had a totally brilliant day, deciding to have lunch out instead of dinner. They'd eaten at the Wight Mouse Inn and spent the afternoon on the west side of the island, bombing down the military road at, like, seventy miles an hour, which was all Dad's old Ford Focus could manage these days. They'd ended up at Freshwater Bay, where they'd wandered down the beach and chucked stones in the water. On the way back, they'd stopped at Mottistone and taken the short walk to see the thirteen-foot Neolithic standing stone there.

Michael had acted all unimpressed, moaning it wasn't exactly Stonehenge. Then he'd pushed Rufus back against it and snogged him silly. He'd have done more, Rufus reckoned, cos he'd started going on about how the stone was just a fucking great dick, yeah, so it was bound to be a fertility symbol, so maybe if he leaned Rufus up against it and shagged him, Michael would get him up the duff, and he'd seemed well up for the attempt. Only just then a couple of elderly ramblers wandered onto the scene, which Rufus and Michael only noticed when the bloke coughed politely and asked them if they'd mind awfully moving over so his wife could take a picture of the stone. So then they'd legged it, laughing, and Michael insisting Dad had to be behind the interruption somehow and probably had spies all over the island.

It'd been *brilliant*.

Rufus was almost sorry to get back to the B&B. Except not really, cos it was definitely a bit nippy once the sun had gone down, and anyway, he had a meal to get ready.

"Dad, we're home," he called out. "Did you get all the shopping?"

Dad's head appeared round the door. Then the rest of him followed. "Ah, Rufus. Yes, although I couldn't get fresh porcini mushrooms"—Rufus tensed—"so I got some dried ones." Rufus relaxed again. He could work with that. After last night's elaborate dinner, he was just doing a simple pasta dish tonight, with a side salad dressed with balsamic vinegar.

"Right, I'll just wash my hands, and I'll get dinner on." He headed straight for the sink.

"Right-oh," Dad said, and disappeared again.

"Um . . ." Michael hung his jacket on the back of a chair and looked awkward. "You want me to, um, peel anything or chop it or whatever?"

Rufus beamed. "You could mince the garlic. You know, if you're not worried a bit of mincing will threaten your masculinity."

"Eff off." Michael glanced at the door. Maybe he didn't want Dad or Shelley to catch him swearing.

Bless.

"So where's this garlic mincer, then?" Michael carried on, opening and closing cupboards. "What does it even look like?"

Rufus stared at him. "Um, like this?" He held up the appropriate article.

Michael frowned at it. "That's a knife."

"Well done. Go to the top of the class. Excellent skills in utensil recognition."

Michael raised an eyebrow. "Any more of that and I'll demonstrate my skills in shoving utensils where the sun don't shine. Seriously, you expect me to use *that*? It looks like something you'd use to gut a bloody zombie."

"What are you, stupid? Everyone knows you have to go for their brains or they just keep coming. And yes, this is what you use to mince garlic."

"But it's fucking enormous."

Rufus smirked. "That's what *he* said."

"In your dreams, pretty boy. Wanna get out a ruler? We all know who'd win a dick-measuring—"

He broke off as Shelley wandered in, carrying a couple of dirty mugs. Luckily, she seemed a bit dreamy and like she hadn't heard what Michael just said. She stopped in her tracks when she saw Rufus and Michael, and frowned. "Everything all right in here, boys?"

To be fair on her, Rufus *was* waving an eight-inch stainless-steel blade at Michael at the time. "We're fine, thanks. Just getting started on dinner."

She still didn't look convinced. "Do you want me to take Michael off your hands?"

Over Rufus's dead body. And probably Dad's as well. "No, thanks. He's helping," Rufus added proudly.

"He's gonna teach me how to mince," Michael put in sourly.

Shelley smiled. "That'll be nice. Rufus is really good at that. Want me to do anything to help?"

"No," Rufus and Michael both said at once.

"Oh. Okay. I'll go and have a sit down with your dad, then."

CHAPTER 13
LOLLOP

Dinner was fucking amazing. Again. Michael wondered if he could get the recipe off Rufus for his mum—but nah, no point. He'd never seen her use fresh garlic in his life, and as far as she was concerned, a mushroom was a mushroom, and she didn't hold with them having weird names and giving themselves airs. Good, plain food, that was what his mum liked to cook. And yeah, she was great at it—no one was allowed to knock Michael's mum's cooking—but maybe it did get a bit samey after a while, the whole meat-and-two-veg thing. Michael liked potatoes as much as the next man, but he was starting to think maybe he didn't need to have them in some form *every* meal.

Now, Rufus's food . . . Yeah, it was a faff, and he'd moaned the whole time when Rufus was getting all finicky about how fine he chopped the garlic, but even he could taste the difference between the end result and the sort of thing Mum produced with her jar of garlic powder. He'd never really got the whole post-shag downer thing—he always felt fucking fantastic after he'd just come—but swallowing the last forkful of Rufus's pasta gave him a whole new understanding of the concept.

Michael was glad they'd already shagged, cos seriously, if he'd only just met Rufus, he'd have thought the bloke was well out of his league with a talent like that.

"Oi, Rufe, why are you not working as head chef in some posh London restaurant?"

Rufus glanced at his dad. "Uh . . ."

"You oughtta be cooking for royalty, not plebs like me," Michael went on, cos seriously, it was like a tragedy or something.

"There's a lot to be said for staying at home," Gerald said. "Although you're quite right, Rufus could go straight to the top if he wanted to. We're just lucky he's chosen to remain here."

Shelley looked up from her salad. "Yeah, it's such a shame—"

"Could you pass the wine, please?" Rufus interrupted her. "Thanks, Dad. Shelley, do you want a top-up?"

"I shouldn't, but oh, go on." She held out her glass.

"Yeah, me too." Michael drained his glass and shoved it under Rufus's nose before they could finish it off between them. He wasn't much of a wine drinker, but this stuff was all right. Not all sweet like his mum's Liebfraumilch, which was a crap name for a wine anyhow. His middle sister Hope had done German at school, and she'd told him it meant *love woman milk*, which sounded a bit dirty if you asked him.

"We're going to need another bottle," Shelley said. "Gerald, would you, love?"

"Yes, of course." Gerald got up and disappeared into the kitchen, coming back a minute later with the goods.

"That's better," Shelley said. "Now, what was I talking about?"

Maybe Rufus didn't hear her, cos he burst straight in with "Michael used to stay on the island when he was a kid," and then they all got talking about chalets versus caravans and how you didn't wanna stay in the holiday camp up by the Needles these days, what with how half of it had fallen into the sea. Which was all kinds of disturbing, cos the more they described it, the more Michael was convinced he had actually stayed there one time.

He was gonna have nightmares tonight. He could tell.

They went for a walk after they'd eaten, just him and Rufus. Down to the seafront and along the prom, all lit up with street lamps and reminding Michael vaguely of a trip to Blackpool Illuminations when he'd been little. He'd almost forgotten that ever happened.

He wasn't sure, but he reckoned he'd eaten too much ice cream and thrown up on the tram.

"Jesus, you trying to bring back bad memories for me?" Michael protested once he realised they were heading towards the pier.

"What, of meeting me? Thanks."

As if. "Any time. Nah, seriously, you got any idea how crap it was, getting shoved in the sea like that? The water was fucking freezing. Half the bloody Atlantic Ocean went up my nose."

He'd been expecting some sympathy, maybe even a "poor baby," but Rufus was frowning. "I thought you said you'd jumped?"

Shit. "No, wait, *you* said I'd jumped. I didn't say nothing. It was Trix, right? She got in a snit when I broke up with her, din't she?"

"And she pushed you in the sea? Poor baby."

"*Finally* I get some sympathy here."

"Not you. Her. She must have been really upset."

"Oi! *I* was sodding upset about it and all." Especially when he'd seen the mess she'd made of his stuff.

Rufus bit his lip, which was well cute and made Michael wanna forgive him. Jesus, he was gonna have to watch all these mushy feelings. "Were you going out with her long?"

Michael shrugged. "Only a few weeks."

"And you came on holiday with her?" Rufus's tone was disbelieving.

Michael felt a bit defensive. It wasn't *that* weird. "It was Trix's idea. Thought it'd be a laugh, din't I? And it's not like we went to Outer fucking Mongolia. If it didn't work out, I could just go home."

"Except you met me," Rufus said, all smiles again.

Michael wanted to hug him, but that not-too-far-from-home thing cut both ways. "Yeah," he said, and gave Rufus a friendly shove instead, which led to Rufus shoving him back and them getting into a bit of a tussle (which *wasn't* the thing on the end of his mum's curtain tie-backs, he'd found out from his calendar a week ago Wednesday), and nearly knocking over an old lady walking her dogs, which did a good job of getting rid of the stiffy Michael had been getting from all the messing about.

They apologised, sat the old dear down on a nearby bench, and chatted about her grandkids for a bit to calm her down. She had three, with two of 'em roughly the same age as Faith's eldest, so Michael was able to give her some pointers for birthday presents, which he wrote down for her cos she'd come out without her glasses.

"That was really nice of you," Rufus said after they'd waved good-bye and walked off side by side with no messing about this time.

"What was?" Michael was busy brushing sandy paw prints off his jeans.

"You know. Spending all that time with her."

Michael shoved his hands in his pockets. "Yeah, well. Old ladies don't get listened to much. There's an old biddy next door to Mum's I do a bit of gardening for—I mean, it's not like it's any extra effort when I'm doing ours anyhow—and every time I go round she always says it's the first conversation she's had all day that wasn't with her cats."

Rufus gave him a soppy smile. "You're just a total sweetie under that rough, gruff exterior, aren't you?" He slipped his hand in Michael's arm.

"Shut up," Michael muttered, embarrassed, and pulled away to jump up on the low wall and look out to sea. "'S France that way, innit? You ever been over there?"

"No—you?"

"Nah. Weird, innit? I've been to Spain, Greece, and a couple of other places, but never to the country next door. You get over to Southampton much?" Michael asked, cos it was sort of on topic and a lot more relevant to his interests than whether Rufus went on foreign holidays.

Rufus didn't answer for a mo. "Um. Not a lot, lately."

"S'pose you never had a good reason to, eh?" Michael said with a leer, jumping back down. "What about gay bars, then? There's none over here. I checked."

"When?" Rufus asked as they walked on.

"Before I came, obviously." Cos he still hadn't sorted out his phone, which for all he knew was dead as a fucking dodo after whatever Trix had done to it.

From the whiff of the water that'd dripped out of it, he had a nasty suspicion she'd dropped it down the bog. And peed on it.

Rufus gave him a level look. "So while you were packing to come away with your *girlfriend*, you went online to see if there was anywhere you'd be able to pick up men? Did you come here planning to split up with her? And wouldn't it have been cheaper, not to mention kinder, to do it at home?"

"Oi, I didn't come here *to* break up with her. It just happened, all right? I realised it wasn't gonna work, so I, you know. Broke it to her gently. And seriously, why are we even talking about this? You always spend your time out with a bloke talking about his exes?"

"Well, sometimes, yeah. Like I said, it's not a big dating pool on the island. It's always good to find out if you've got someone in common."

Michael laughed. "What, so you can bond over what a tit he was? So go on then, tell me about your exes."

"You *really* want to know?" Rufus started counting on his fingers. "Well, first there was Andrew Harding, when we were at school. We just kissed, really. I mean, I tried to give him a blowjob once, but he, um, came before I could get my mouth on it. Then there was a bit of a break, cos Mum was ill and I didn't feel like going out much." He stared out to sea for a mo, blinking.

Shit, Michael wanted to hold him. He put a hand on Rufus's shoulder, which seemed to rouse him out of wherever he'd buggered off to.

"Then there was Dyl, but we broke up when he went off to uni. So if I'm planning to carry on the family tradition, we should be getting back together in around eight years or so. And then there was Adam. And now you."

"What happened to Adam?"

"He was the tit."

"Couldn't keep it in his pants?"

"Don't think he knew where his pants *were*, half the time." Rufus looked lost in memory, and it was a fucking awful memory at that.

"Bastard." Sod it. There was no one much around. Michael gave Rufus a quick hug to get rid of the sad face. Yeah, that was much better. Then he frowned. "Oi, what about Simon?"

"Who?"

"'S what you yelled out that first time when I got you off."

"No, I didn't."

"Yeah, you did. Or something like it. P'simon? Whatever the fuck kind of name that is?"

"Oh. That. It was, um, Poseidon. You know, Greek god Poseidon?"

"Uh-huh." Michael smirked. "Got a thing for Greek gods, have you? So Percy Jackson films are like total wank fodder for you, yeah?"

"Um, yeah, well, not all of them. It's just, Poseidon's like god of the sea, and you came out of the sea, so I was sort of saying thanks . . ." Rufus trailed off at Michael's look, which was fair enough because bloody hell, this was cracking him up.

And yeah, it was pretty cute too. Christ, Michael had never met anyone like Rufus before. He wasn't even sure there *was* anyone like Rufus.

"Oh, look," Rufus said brightly. "We're nearly at the pier. Do you want to go up it?"

"Not a lot, no." Michael shivered inside his jacket. "It's getting a bit nippy."

"Right, this way, then." Rufus led him up a steep side street, away from the pier. "Want to go for a drink somewhere?"

Michael couldn't see the point. He wanted to get laid, not wasted. "Nah, why don't we head back to the B&B?" He grinned. "We could do something to warm up there."

"I'm not having sex with you with Dad and Shelley in the house."

Shit. You had to admire the bloke for sticking to his guns—well, most of Michael did, but his dick was less than impressed. "That's crazy. You had sex with me in that shack where anyone could have seen us."

"Yeah, but not Dad and Shelley."

"How d'you know? They could've come up to check on your dad's mate's place or something."

"No, they couldn't. We had the car, remember?" They turned the corner, which meant they'd now be walking downhill, thank God. Michael liked to think he was pretty fit, but they'd done a lot of walking today and that hill had been bloody steep.

He didn't realise until too late that Rufus was leading him back down the high street. Bugger. That'd take them right past him and Trix's hotel. Still, what were the odds they'd run into—

Fuck. There she was. Judy the judgemental receptionist, coming straight towards them. Michael thought fast and dragged Rufus into the nearest doorway. Then he snogged the crap out of him.

A couple of passing cars honked their horns, and someone yelled out "Poofters!" which, yeah, obviously he hadn't *quite* thought this through. Michael cringed inside but carried on with the lip-lock, cos if he stopped now it'd be even worse.

He just hoped Judy wouldn't realise it was him—far as she knew, he was straight. So with a bit of luck she'd just walk on by without saying anything he wouldn't want Rufus to hear. Rufus had already been a bit too keen to see Trix's side of things. If he found out she'd just proposed to Michael when he dumped her . . . Well. Not that Michael thought he'd done anything wrong—for Christ's sake, how was he supposed to know she was gonna do that?—but he could see how, if you put the wrong sort of spin on it, he might not come out of it all smelling like roses. More like raw sewage.

Michael *really* didn't want Rufus to start thinking of him as a big, steaming pile of shit. He shivered.

Rufus seemed to like that, and held him tighter. Okay, this was getting to be a problem, because that stiffy was back with a vengeance. He risked a look over his shoulder, and was in luck—Judy's pert little tight-skirted bum was wiggling its way up the high street, away from them. Thank God.

"Why'd you stop?" Rufus asked, sounding breathless. Score one for Michael.

"Coast's clear," he said without thinking.

"What coast?"

Shit. Although, looking on the bright side, the stiffy was no longer a problem. "Uh, them gits what were heckling us. But maybe we oughtta get outta here in case they decide to come back and give us a kicking?"

"Yeah, guess so. Um. Give me a mo." Rufus glanced around nervously before adjusting himself in his jeans.

Score two for Michael.

"Okay," Rufus went on. "I'm good."

"Good? You're fucking perfect," Michael said, cos he liked to see Rufus smile. And fuck it, maybe it was true, at that.

Course, once they got back to the B&B, that was the end of their alone time. Despite Rufus's dad having theoretically given his blessing for them to . . . Actually, come to think of it, all he'd given his blessing to was Rufus taking Michael out on a sight-seeing tour. Yeah, the evening made a lot more sense once Michael had remembered that. Whatever room in the place they tried hanging out in (kitchen, guests' living room, etc., etc.) they ended up getting cockblocked when Gerald turned up to do some apparently vital bit of household maintenance. Although he was clearly running out of ideas by the end of the evening. He used the "radiator needs bleeding" excuse two rooms in a row.

That night, Michael lay in bed, gave his dick a quick tug, and wondered whether to jerk off or try to make it across the hall to Rufus's room. Which, yeah, would be much more fun, but was it worth the risk? His dick definitely thought so, but the rest of him wasn't so sure. His feet were a bit tender after all the walking they'd done today, and he didn't fancy getting any more bruises. Not to mention making a right tit of himself in front of Shelley and Gerald.

Then his door opened, and Rufus slipped inside, looking like a fucking wet dream in boxer briefs and a T-shirt. He pulled the shirt over his head and chucked it on the floor before climbing into bed with Michael, who could hardly believe his luck.

"Survived your dad's booby traps, then?" he asked, grabbing handfuls of Rufus and pulling him close.

Rufus nuzzled into Michael's neck. "It was easy. I don't think his heart was really in it tonight. Just a couple of trip wires and some drawing pins outside your door."

"You're joking, right?" Christ, if Michael needed a pee in the night, he was doing it in the sink. "Hey, what happened to you insisting we're not doing it with your parents in the house? Not that I'm complaining, mind." He gave Rufus's arse a good squeeze in happy anticipation.

Rufus pushed himself up on his arms and stared down at Michael. "We're still not doing it. I just thought it'd be nice to have a bit of a cuddle."

Well, shit. "What? I don't cuddle, all right? Not with blokes." It was true. None of the other blokes he'd been with had been into all that soft stuff.

"What, cos cuddling a girl is more manly, somehow? That's just daft. Anyway, we've cuddled loads already. What about in the Love Shack?"

"It's different if you've just shagged. It's . . . I dunno. Natural. Hormones make you do it. And anyway, how am I s'posed to relax with this?" He ground his hard-on into Rufus's side and gave him his best seductive smile for good measure.

Result. He could *see* Rufus weakening.

"C'mon," he said in his lowest, roughest voice. "I'll be quiet. And I'll *definitely* make it worth your while."

Rufus bit his lip and looked over his shoulder at the door. Michael took the chance to get his hand down the front of those boxer briefs and give him a gentle squeeze where it'd do most good.

Rufus whimpered. "I'm not gonna be able to keep quiet," he moaned.

"So? Door's locked." Michael gave Rufus a look. "You *did* lock the door behind you just now, yeah?"

"Um. Probably not. Maybe I should . . ."

"You're staying right there." Michael got out of bed and locked the door himself, cos with Rufus doing his scaredy-cat act again, Michael wouldn't put it past him to get cold feet halfway there and use the door instead of locking it.

Then he got back into bed, savouring the moment.

"Um, I still don't think we ought to . . . I don't want them to hear," Rufus whispered, his gaze firmly on Michael's dick, which, to be fair, had chubbed up nicely and was now bobbing along in front of his eyes as Michael knelt up over him.

Michael grinned. "You don't need to worry about that. I've got just the thing to keep you quiet."

Later, well-shagged and happy with a passed-out Rufus making cute little snuffly noises in his arms, Michael tried to stop the voices in his head. It'd just been a practical solution to the noise problem, all right? Making sure neither of them got too loud when they got off. Sensible, even.

Just cos he'd done sixty-nine with a bloke for the first time *definitely* didn't mean he was gay.

So that was all right. Michael drifted off to sleep, dreaming of him and Rufus having their own little love shack on the mainland. Preferably with four walls and zero risk of arrest, but hey, he wasn't picky.

CHAPTER 14
LURCH

Of course, Michael might have known that next morning it'd all go tits up. Not right away, mind—waking up with Rufus had been pretty fucking awesome, even if they hadn't got up to much cos of Rufus getting another attack of paranoia. It was just nice, all right, waking up to that cute little face and fluffy-chick bed hair.

Shut up.

Michael could appreciate stuff, couldn't he? It didn't mean he was going soft or nothing.

They'd got dressed and were leaning against the kitchen counters, mugs of tea in hand, discussing what to do for the day. Shelley was there too, sitting at the table with her nose in a magazine, and Gerald was off doing . . . old-man stuff, what the fuck ever, Michael had no clue.

Michael, as always, was the voice of reason. "It's an island, yeah? Surrounded by water. So we oughtta do something, you know, related to that."

"Yeah, but we did the beach yesterday," Rufus said. "I think I pulled a muscle in my stone-throwing arm. We should—"

"Not the beach," Michael corrected him, scratching his armpit thoughtfully. "The water, right? We can do something on the water."

Rufus glanced at his stepmum, but she didn't look up from the latest *EastEnders* cast scandal. "Um, right, yeah, but, see, there's this castle, too? Carisbrooke. Right in the middle, and I read this book where someone tried to kill the hero by pushing him down the stairs there, so we should totally—"

Jesus. Talk about people who didn't *listen*. "I wanna do a boat trip, all right? Round the Needles or out to one of them forts they built to stop Napoleon. I know it's off-season but come on, there's more boats on this island than people. There's gotta be someone who'll take us out if we pay 'em."

"Oh, you won't get Rufus on a boat," Shelley butted in, putting down her magazine. "He's got a phobia. Can't even get on the Isle of Wight ferry without having a panic attack, poor love." She half stood to reach for the biscuit tin, stopped, patted her hip with a grimace, and sat back down at the table to carry on with her morning fix of celebrity gossip.

Michael was left staring at Rufus in disbelief. "You're telling me you live on an island, and you're scared of the water?"

Rufus went pink. "I'm not scared of water. Water is fine, as long as it stays where it's supposed to. I just don't want to go out on it in a boat, that's all."

Michael frowned. "So how do you cope when you have to go to the mainland?"

Looked like Rufus *really* liked those Crocs of his, cos he just gazed down at them and didn't say anything.

Shit. "Are you trying to tell me you've never been off the Isle of Wight? *Seriously?*"

"I've *been* off," Rufus said defensively. "Just not that recently."

"How recently?"

Rufus muttered something to his Crocs.

"Oi, so I can hear it, yeah?"

"Look, just don't laugh, all right? Six years ago. I mean, I tried the following year, but that was when I got the panic attack." He glanced over at Shelley.

She smiled. "Yeah, that's right. Your dad told me all about it. Speaking of which, I'd better take him his tea before it gets cold, the silly old bugger." Shelley ambled out, her magazine under her arm and a mug in each hand.

Michael wasn't laughing. He'd never felt *less* like laughing. "So when I gave you my number, and said call me when you're in Southampton, that was basically never gonna happen?"

"Um..."

"And all this, this 'try having a boyfriend, see how you like it, we're only a few miles apart as the crow flies,' it was all a load of bollocks, wasn't it? We might as well be fucking *continents* apart. You seriously expect me to hop on a fucking ferry every time I fancy a shag? When you're never gonna meet me halfway?"

Rufus gave an awkward little laugh. "That'd be the middle of the Solent. I don't think it'd work."

"This isn't a fucking joke!" Michael couldn't *believe* it. He'd actually started to think maybe him and Rufus could work out, could have something...

"Let's go outside for a minute, yeah?" Rufus whispered.

"Fuck that," Michael said. "Look—"

He broke off as Gerald strode in, frowning. "I've just been having a very interesting telephone conversation with Judy from the Selsey Hotel," he said, glaring straight at Michael. "Specifically, concerning the abysmal way you treated the young lady you came to the island with."

Jesus fucking Christ. He did *not* need this. No way. Not any time, but definitely not *now*. "Lemme guess. You're chucking me out. Fine. I'll save you the bother. I'm going. I'll get my bag and I'll be outta your way." He slammed down his mug and stomped towards the stairs.

"Michael—" Rufus made a move to follow him, but his dad held him back.

Fine.

Just fucking fine.

It didn't take long to shove the last of his crap in his bag, which still reeked of shampoo. Michael grabbed his jacket and stormed back down the stairs.

Rufus was standing at the bottom, wide-eyed, his dad hovering a few feet away. "Is it true? Judy told Dad you let your girlfriend bring you on a romantic holiday, and then you were a total shit to her. She said she actually asked you to *marry* her and you basically just told her to sod off."

He'd just fucking *known* she'd put the worst possible spin on it, and of *course* they'd believe her word over his. Bastards. "So? What gives *you* the right to get on my case about it, anyway? It's not like we had a sodding *relationship* or anything, is it, Mr. Forgot-to-mention-I-never-leave-the-fucking-island. How the hell did you think that was gonna work?"

That was the worst bit. He'd let Michael get all . . . *whatever* . . . without ever once telling him, *Oh, by the way, us being together has got about as much chance of working out as a twenty-year-old refurbed Hotpoint has of winning an award for energy efficiency.* The fact *they* were getting on *his* case now about Trix was just the rancid fucking cherry on top of . . . of . . . whatever the fuck people put cherries on top of, Christ, *he* didn't know. And he didn't fucking care, either.

Rufus darted a glance over his shoulder at his dad. "I thought you could come over at weekends and stuff?" he said in a small voice.

Michael snorted. "Yeah, cos the welcome around here's so fucking *warm*. I'll see you around. *If* you ever get the balls to get on a ferry." He pushed past Rufus and went out the front door, slamming it behind him.

Fury carried him halfway up the high street, where he hit pay dirt in the form of a taxi rank with a couple of cars in it. "Southampton ferry, yeah?" he said to the driver of the one in front, and slung his bag in the back.

CHAPTER 15
SHAKE

Michael had just . . . left. Rufus couldn't believe what was happening. Had happened. Past tense. Done. Dusted.

Fucked up beyond all hope of recovery.

He stared at the front door. Was it his imagination or was it still vibrating from the force of Michael's anger?

Rufus just couldn't believe his life had gone from positively perfect to fatally fucked up in, like, an *instant*. Less than an instant. A nano-instant. A pico-instant, even.

"Dad?" he said in a voice that sounded like it could have belonged to *any* kid who'd just passed his fifth birthday.

Dad pulled him into a one-armed hug. "There, there," he said, sounding uncomfortable but determined. "I'm sure it's all for the best. I don't think he was the sort of person you could have been happy with."

"Oh, love." Shelley came and hugged him on the other side. Rufus blinked rapidly. He was *not* going to cry.

Shelley was still speaking. "I couldn't believe it when Gerald told me what he'd done to that poor young woman. He seemed like such a nice young man."

"But . . ." Rufus struggled to make his voice work properly. "He said him and Trix had only been together a couple of weeks."

Dad shook his head. "I don't think that can be true. Why would she propose after only a couple of weeks? Why would they even go on holiday together after so short a time?"

"I don't know! Maybe she's the love-at-first-sight type? Or she, like, got to know him a bit and then just knew she didn't want to risk him getting away. Ever? I mean, I *know* that happens." Rufus's face went hot, and he hurried on. "Maybe she's always just *really* wanted to get married? You didn't even give him a chance to explain!"

"Now, that's not true, love," Shelley said, stroking Rufus's hair. "It was him what stormed off like that. We'd of listened to him, wouldn't we, love?"

Dad coughed. "Yes, of course. Quite unreasonable of him, really. As if he was just looking for an excuse."

Oh god. So it *was* Rufus's fault he'd gone. "It's cos of me not wanting to leave the island," he told his Crocs.

"Think so, love." Shelley put her head on his shoulder, which was at least less painful than the knife she'd just shoved in his heart. "Think he thought you'd be the one going to see him all the time. And that's not fair, is it?"

"Yeah, but . . . neither is me expecting him to come over here all the time, is it?" He'd been so *stupid*.

"You can't help having a phobia," Shelley said angrily.

Rufus's insides felt all hot and prickly.

"And the last thing you need," Dad chimed in, "is someone who's not prepared to show some basic understanding of your situation. Or hold a reasonable, balanced discussion on the matter."

"Why would you want to be going over to the mainland all the time, anyway? You're happy here, aren't you, love?" Shelley asked.

Rufus nodded. He didn't trust himself to speak.

"Of course you are," Dad said. "I know we both hoped you'd have a career as a chef, but, well, perhaps things have turned out for the best. You know I'd have struggled to manage without you since your poor mum died. She'd be so proud, you know, if she could see you now."

Rufus bit his lip. "Think . . . think I wanna be alone for a bit," he managed.

"Course, love," Shelley said, giving him a squeeze. "You take all the time you want."

CHAPTER 16
WAVER

Of course, by the time Michael had got to the ferry terminal, bought a ticket—cos his original return ticket had already left the island when Trix did—and made it through the ferry journey—which seemed to take forever, Christ, how slow could these bloody tin tubs go?—the anger had all gone and left him feeling flat as the surface of the Solent on a still day.

He got a cab back home, suffering through the driver's terminal cheerfulness and chatter, yap yap yap, Christ, was the bloke related to Trix or something? Michael paid him back by giving him the world's stingiest tip. Then he trudged slowly up the garden path and let himself into the boxy council semi he shared with his mum.

She came bustling into the hallway, drying her hands on a tea towel. "Michael? But you're home early."

Michael squirmed, but let her give him a hug and a kiss on the cheek, which she had to stand on tiptoe for. Her hair was its usual red-brown colour, but her roots were showing pure white at her parting. How come he'd never noticed that before?

She really was the same age as Rufus's dad, he realised. He'd just never thought of her as so old.

"It's good to see you back," Mum went on, brushing his hair off his forehead. Michael batted her hand away with a muttered *Mu-um*. "Have you had your lunch? I can make you a bacon sandwich if you like."

"Nah, 's okay. I had some chips on the ferry." It'd been something to do to stop him thinking about Rufus.

"Well, if you're sure you're not hungry? I haven't got a thing in for tea," she said, frowning. "I'll pop to the shops, and then I can make steak and kidney pudding tonight."

"With cheesy mashed potatoes?" Michael asked hopefully. Mum's cheesy mashed potatoes were the *best*.

Rufus probably had a fancy French version he did too . . . But Michael wasn't gonna think about Rufus.

"Of course. Do I ever not?"

Well, there had been that one time, but that was when they'd run out of cheese cos he'd got hungry earlier and made cheese on toast and forgotten to tell her he'd used it all up. "Course not, Mum."

"Now, tell me all about your trip. Did you and Trix not have a good time?"

"Uh, not exactly." Michael grimaced in memory. "We split up."

"Oh, what a shame. Come on into the kitchen and I'll make you a cup of tea."

Mum bustled around with the kettle, limping a bit from the hip she wouldn't go to see the doctor about because she didn't like a fuss. "Still, I'm not sure it's not all for the best," she went on. "I was talking to Di Griffin—you know, from the Co-op?—and *she* told *me* she'd seen that girl holding hands with another young woman. In Marks and Spencer's, of all places! Now, maybe it was all perfectly innocent, but well, I must say, she certainly *looks* like a lesbian. You're not telling me it's natural for a girl to have all those muscles. And so tall!"

Okay, that wasn't fair. "She can't help how tall she is, Mum. That's just genetics."

"You say that, but I've heard some of these women take male hormones. And you can't tell me there's anything natural about *that*."

"Mum, what you're talking about, it's totally different, yeah? And it's all right, anyway. Trix *told* me she was bi."

"It is not all right, Michael O'Grady! I have every sympathy for those poor souls the Lord sees fit to make homosexual—they say it's not a choice, so we have to make allowances for them. But these bisexuals"—she pronounced it *buy-sex-you-alls,* with an emphasis on the *sex*—"have no excuse for that sort of behaviour, do they? Now don't you look at me like that. I'm glad your Trix was trying to do the right thing and find a nice young man to settle down with, but I can't say I'm sorry it's not going to be you. She seemed nice enough"—from Mum, that meant *I knew she was no good, the minute I laid eyes on her, the trollop*—"but, well, with a girl like that, how do you know she won't slip, and go back to her old ways?"

"Mum, it's not like an addiction."

"Then how do you explain all these politicians who get caught consorting with rentboys and the like? They try to do the right thing, but they're not strong enough to resist their . . . *urges.*" Mum shook her head, tight-lipped. Michael tried not to show how uncomfortable she was making him feel. Best to let her get it out of her system.

Until next time.

"I'm just glad you've been spared all of that, for all you seemed so keen on her," Mum carried on and then, thank God, changed the subject. "Now, that's quite enough talking about those sorts of things. What did you do on the island, then? Did you go to see the dinosaurs?"

Michael rolled his eyes. "Mum, I'm not five. And they weren't open anyway."

"Oh, that's a shame. I remember the first time we took your sisters to Blackgang Chine, your dad and I. Way before you were born, of course—Charity had only just started playgroup." Mum stared out of the window with that weird half smile she always got when she talked about his dad. "They had such a lovely time, all of them, climbing up to ride the dinosaurs. And the girls loved the nursery rhymes garden. It just wasn't the same, taking you all there after he'd . . ." She blinked a bit, then shook her head. "Still, all this isn't getting the tea brewed."

"Mum, sit down, yeah? I'll make the tea."

She laughed. "Don't be silly."

"All right, but I'll go to the shops to get stuff for tonight, okay?"

"Michael O'Grady, you'll do no such thing. I am *quite* capable of doing my own shopping."

Michael gave up. "Can you get some rice, then?"

"Rice? I think we might have some in the cupboard, but it's probably out of date. I haven't made rice pudding for ages."

"That'd be perfect, then. It's for my phone. It got wet."

"Oh, Michael. How many times do I have to tell you to be careful with your things?"

"Hey, it wasn't me, all right? Trix, uh, borrowed it and dropped it in the sea." If he told Mum Trix had dropped it in the loo, she'd only want to bleach it or boil it or something.

"She should buy you a new one, then."

"Mum, I'm not gonna go over to my ex-girlfriend's house and demand a new phone, all right? She'd laugh in my face." Or punch it.

"Hmph. In my day people took responsibility for their actions."

"It's only a phone, Mum." Still, it was gonna be a right bugger if it died. Michael hadn't backed up his photos and contacts and stuff for about six months. He still had his work phone up in his bedroom, but all that had on it was work stuff. Obviously. And he never gave out that number, so none of his mates would be able to ring him.

He wondered if Rufus would try to ring him. Maybe he already had?

Shit. There was an ache inside him, a fucking great big empty hole where Rufus had been. He *missed* the lying little bastard.

Still, maybe Mum was right, and it was all for the best.

Even if she had been talking about Trix, not Rufus.

Shit. It'd stop hurting soon.

Wouldn't it?

CHAPTER 17
QUIVER

Being alone, Rufus decided after a quick but intensive wallow in misery under his duvet, really wasn't all it was cracked up to be. What had Garbo been *thinking*?

He reached for his phone and hit Call.

"Whatdjer want, pickle sniffer?"

A cuddle, please. "Liz, where are you?"

"Down at the swings with Kieran. You know, the ones down by the crazy golf. Wanna come push him?"

"See you in ten minutes, yeah?" Rufus scrambled out from under the duvet, jammed his feet in his trainers, and headed off.

There had always been swings down by the crazy golf course, even when Rufus was little—even when his mum and dad had been little, come to think of it—but now there was a proper little playground with bouncy rubber flooring and brightly painted climbing frames meant to look like ships and castles and stuff. Little Kieran was digging away in the sandpit like he was hoping to reach Australia before nap time, bundled up to twice normal size in thick trousers, anorak, and woolly hat. Rufus vaguely remembered his own mum, when he was little, telling him she'd found him under a gooseberry bush. Kieran looked like Liz had found him in the dictionary under the definition of "totes adorbs."

She was sitting on a bench nearby, watching like a hawk ready to swoop with razor-like claws in case any of the other toddlers showed violent intentions towards her pride and joy.

"God, what's happened?" Liz's eyes narrowed as Rufus approached. "I thought something was wrong when you called me 'Liz.' Do I need to sharpen my cleaver?"

Rufus sighed, sitting down next to her. There was plenty of room, although all the other benches had several people sitting on them. Liz tended to have that effect on people, although they'd been working on it for months, and she was showing definite signs of progress. Sometimes she even smiled at the other mums. "No. Maybe. Michael's gone."

"Gone where? Gone home? Gone back to his girlfriend? Gone for a long walk off a short pier—again?"

Rufus looked at her sharply. "Did I tell you about that?"

"No, but I got talking to Amy, Kieran's little mate Jayden's mum, who's mates with Judy at the Selsey—"

"Oh, bloody hell. Why doesn't she just ring up the *County Post* and get them to run the story?"

"What makes you think she hasn't? Anyway, so you dumped him, right? Good for you. I thought he was a bastard."

"I didn't dump him. He just left," Rufus said sadly. "We had a row when he found out about my ferry thing."

"So? Good riddance, if you ask me."

"No! Not good riddance. *Bad* riddance." Rufus gestured wildly and impotently. "I *like* him, all right? What am I going to do?"

Liz looked at him for a long moment. "You're saying you want him back? He's a prick. What sort of bloke treats his girlfriend like that?"

"I don't know! I just don't think it can have been as bad as Judy's been saying. I mean, he told me some of it. Like, he split up with this Trix girl and she got upset and pushed him off the pier."

"And then went straight round to yours and shagged the pants off you. He's a shit."

Well, yeah, but— "No one's listening to his side of the story!"

"They can't, can they? Cos he's buggered off." She was silent for a mo. "So what did you tell him about your ferry thing, anyhow?"

"I didn't. Shelley told him."

"That's not good."

"I know. I know, all right? And I never got a chance to *say* anything. I mean, without Shelley or Dad there."

"I told you that one was gonna come back to bite you on the bum. I *told* you."

"Yeah, well, it was already too late then, wasn't it? I'd been, like, *living* it for years before we even met."

"So what are you gonna do?"

"Don't know."

"Have you tried ringing him?"

"His phone's off. Probably permanently. His ex did a number on it. Pun not intended."

She frowned at him. "What?"

"Forget it. So I've got, like, *no* way of getting in touch."

"Hmm . . ." Liz pursed her lips. "What about Judy? She might have his address. You take an address when people book at the B&B, right? As opposed to just turning up on your doorstep saying 'Oi, gizza room?'"

Rufus's heart leaped. "Yes! Liz, you're brilliant. I'll go round right now and ask her."

"No, you won't. I'll go, and you can mind Kieran for me."

"Why?"

"Roo, think it through. She's so worried about you hanging around with this bloke, she shopped him to your dad. You *really* think she's gonna help you get back together?"

"So why'll she tell you?"

"Easy. I'll say I wanna send him hate mail for hurting my mate. It won't even be a lie, cos if he does turn out to be as big of a shit as everyone except *you* thinks he is, I'll be emptying Kieran's potty into a padded envelope and sending it to him first class." She paused, looking thoughtful. "Or maybe second class. Give the smell a chance to really develop. Anyway, you stay here and do *not* take your eyes of Kieran for a *second*, yeah?"

"Got it." Rufus gave her a jaunty salute that was at total odds with the way he actually felt.

By the time Liz came back, Rufus was covered in sand, his arms were aching from pushing Kieran on the swings, and he had a grazed knee from jumping off the roundabout without due care and attention. But at least he was feeling a bit better about life.

Liz eyed his sweaty, dishevelled state with approval. "You want the good news or the bad news?"

Rufus sat down on the bench, panting, while Kieran slurped on a carton of juice. Some kids got all the luck. "Good. I want good news." He was determined to clutch at every single straw that floated his way.

"Well, I got an address."

"Yay!" Rufus punched the air.

"But it's not Michael's address."

"Poop."

"It's his girlfriend's address."

"Explosive diarrhoea-type poop."

"Poop! Poop! Poop!" a passing tot yelled. Her mum glared at Rufus.

Liz glared back on his behalf. The mum picked up her daughter and hurried away.

"Still, look on the bright side," Liz said, smiling smugly. "At least you and her have got something in common. You've both been dumped by that shithead."

"Let me guess—Judy had a few things to say about Michael when you went round?"

"And some suggestions as to what to send him in the mail. She's really quite creative when you get to know her."

"So what am I supposed to do with the ex's address? Write her a letter and say *I'd* like to send Michael some hate mail?"

Liz shook her head. "She'd just ignore it. I mean, I would. You could be any sleazeball nutjob. Like *him*. No, you gotta have the personal touch. I had this idea while I was walking back. We could kill two birds with one stone."

"You're not still talking about things to do to Michael, are you?" Rufus asked nervously.

"Sort of. But not like that. Look, you and I both know your ferry thing isn't really a thing, right? Don't you think it's time you told your dad the truth?"

"Hmm, let me see . . . How about *no*? Liz, I can't leave the island. What'd Dad do without me?"

"I dunno—employ someone he'd actually have to pay?"

"You know the B&B doesn't make enough money. I mean, it's fine for us all to live on, but not enough to pay someone's rent and stuff. It's like you not being able to work cos you can't afford childcare."

"Yeah, I know, I know. But I'm not asking you to move off, am I? I'm only asking you to go on a flippin' day trip. Look, Michael found out about your ferry thing, right? And that's why he got in a huff and flounced out."

"Michael would never, ever be seen flouncing. But yeah."

"So if you go over there and get his address from the ex, then turn up on his doorstep, that'll prove your thing isn't a thing, won't it? Go on. It's a leap year, innit? You told me leap years are for trying something different. So try it."

"It's not . . ." Rufus screwed up his face. "It's difficult, all right? If Dad finds out I'm not really scared of boats, he's gonna start up again with all the *don't waste your life here, I'll be fine* stuff."

"He'd have a point. That catering course we did, you were streets ahead of everyone else at cooking. The rest of us just took the course cos it seemed like a good bet in a place with so many hotels. If I had your talent, I wouldn't be sitting around wasting it, kid or no kid."

"Yeah, but if I go off to London or Southampton or even just *Ventnor* to train as a chef—"

"Which you could easily do, right, cos it's not like the island hasn't got any decent restaurants, even if you would get stuck with doing seafood, which is totally gross, jeez, who decided just cos you live near the sea, you have to eat every slimy thing that slithers out of it—"

"—Dad *won't* be fine," Rufus interrupted right back. "It'll be just him and Shelley running the B&B. How long do you reckon that's going to last before they go bankrupt or she leaves him or both? That's why he's got to think I can't leave the island. I mean, if I'm going to be stuck here anyway, I might as well work at the B&B, so he doesn't have to feel guilty about it. But if he knows I can go *anywhere . . .*"

Liz drew in a deep breath, opened her mouth—then shut it again. She paused for a moment, then finally spoke. "Fine. So don't tell him."

"What?"

"Don't tell him. You just say you and me are going over to the other side of the island to, I dunno, walk across Tennyson Down or something—I mean, it's not like you're gonna be needed at the B&B,

is it? Your only guest just left—and then we get on the ferry and go over to Southampton. It's not that complicated."

"What about Kieran?"

"I'll sort something out."

"When?"

"Soon as I can. I'll let you know, yeah?"

CHAPTER 18
WOBBLE

Dreams were bastards. See, in Michael's dreams, yeah, he'd been back on the island. Waking up with Rufus in his arms. Rufus was making that cute little snuffly sound and clinging on to him like a sex-starved limpet.

Then he awoke for real, and he was in his old bed in the house he'd grown up in. Alone. Unless you counted the stiffy he'd woken up with, but fuck it, even wanking wasn't much fun today.

After the most pathetic orgasm in the history of self-abuse, Michael cleaned himself off, chucked on some clothes, and trudged down to the kitchen. Mum was in there doing something at the sink.

If Judy hadn't shot her mouth off, Michael could've been doing *Rufus* at the sink back on the island right now. Well, if he'd managed to persuade Rufus's stepmum and dad to leave 'em alone for five minutes. Or even if not, they could be cuddled up somewhere, or Michael could be watching him cook another gourmet breakfast and teasing him about how nipping out to a café for a sausage sarnie would take half the time.

Christ, he missed the little twat. Michael pulled out a chair with an ear-splitting scrape of leg on floor.

Mum turned. "Oh, Michael, you're up. Let me get you some breakfast. Bacon and eggs?"

"Yeah. S'pose." Then he felt guilty. "Oi, why don't you let me do it?"

Mum actually laughed. "That's a kind thought, but I like my pans without the bottoms burned out. You just sit down, and I'll have it ready for you in a jiffy."

"I can do it," he protested. "How hard can it be?"

Mum just laughed again, shook her head, and cracked some eggs into the frying pan. Michael sighed, resigned, and picked up the *Daily Mail*. His calendar's word for the day had been "schadenfreude," and he reckoned the papers would be good for a bit of that.

He still hadn't found anything to make himself feel better about life by the time Mum served up, though, and he set to, but found his appetite waning (yesterday's word; he'd caught up on his reading for the days he'd been away) as he ate. There was nothing *wrong* with Mum's bacon and eggs—well, the yolks were a bit overdone, and the bacon rind had some soggy bits, instead of being uniformly crisp and golden, but that was how she always did them. But somehow it just tasted flat after Rufus's eggs from happy hens and, for all Michael knew, bacon from pigs on ecstasy.

And how come Rufus knew how to cook, and Michael had never learned the first thing? He swallowed his mouthful and put his fork down. "Mum, why did you never get me to help in the kitchen when I was a kid?"

"You were always so much happier kicking a ball around."

"Yeah, but so were the girls, and you always made them do their bit."

"That's different."

"Why? Why is it different?"

"It just is, Michael." She sighed. "Your father, God rest him, wouldn't have wanted you stuck in the kitchen when you could be outside in the fresh air, now would he?"

"I dunno. Maybe he'd have liked me not to starve if I had to fend for myself?"

"And why would you have to do that? I know I'm not going to be here forever, but you'll find a nice girl some day and settle down."

"Mum, I don't think nice girls these days stay nice if you expect them to do all the cooking." He hesitated. "And anyway, what if I . . . don't meet a nice girl?"

"Don't be daft. A handsome young man like you, with a good job? And you've never had any trouble in the past." Mum heaved herself down into the chair next to his and patted his arm. "Don't be discouraged by what happened with Trix. She wasn't the girl for you."

"Maybe . . . maybe there isn't a girl for me?" Shit, this was hard. He wasn't even sure why he was doing it, 'cept . . . it'd hurt, what she'd been saying about bisexuals yesterday. He couldn't help thinking about Rufus, and his dad's easy acceptance of him being gay.

Must be good, knowing your folks loved you for who you were, not who they wanted you to be.

Mum *tutted*. "What did I just tell you? You'll find her. Now, you finish up your breakfast before it gets cold."

Michael gave up.

Michael went for a drive after breakfast. Being around Mum was making him feel uncomfortable and guilty. He needed to get out. And in any case, the Saab had been sitting outside the house for days, not being driven. He didn't wanna end up with a flat battery, did he?

The day was cold but sunny, so Michael thought *Sod it* and put the top down. He didn't have a hat with him, but it never got cold enough for frostbite in Britain, and who needed ears, anyway?

It was fucking exhilarating, bombing along back lanes and through the New Forest. Even if he did have to keep slowing down so as not to *splat* the ponies. Somehow, he ended up driving through Lymington to the coast, parking the car, and getting out to gaze across the Solent to the Isle of Wight. It looked almost close enough to touch from here, the chalk stacks of the Needles clearly visible—and the ferry was only a couple of miles away from where he'd parked. He could get a ticket, go across, and . . .

And what? Find out Rufus still hated him? Even if by some miracle he didn't, Michael would still be stuck with a bloke he'd never get to see. And Christ, it wasn't like he even *wanted* a sodding boyfriend. Things were so much simpler when he just went out with girls.

There were a couple of girls giving him the eye right now, in fact. They were perched on a rock near where he stood, huddled close either for warmth or for maximum gossip and giggle potential. They were in their early twenties, he reckoned, and both were pretty good-looking, at least as far as he could tell under all the layers they had on. Michael shivered, reminded he hadn't dressed for sea breezes.

The girls giggled some more. "Come over here and we'll warm you up," one of them called out to him. They looked all right—up for a bit of a laugh, and not too tarty in the way they dressed. Mum would probably love it if he brought one of them home.

With a weird feeling in his guts like it'd been too long since breakfast, Michael flashed them a smile and shook his head.

Then he walked back to his car.

Thursday nights were kickboxing nights, but Michael decided discretion was the better part of not getting his bollocks kicked in on the off chance Trix turned up. The mood he was in, he probably wasn't safe to spar with anyway. He couldn't help thinking of those girls down by the coast, and it made him fucking mad. They could have been total slappers, shoplifters, benefit cheats, whatever. How fair was it that he could've taken either one of them home, but not the bloke he lo—not Rufus, who was the most selfless person he'd ever met?

He thought about heading down the pub, but, well, people would wonder why he was there on a Thursday, and anyway, too pissed off to risk fighting was probably too pissed off to be drinking. He wasn't worried about turning into a violent drunk—Michael didn't do that—but sobbing his heart out in front of everyone would be well embarrassing.

Besides, if he went to his local, the Pig and Whistle, Gaz would probably be behind the bar, and him and Gaz had a sort of thing where if neither of 'em had a girl, they often ended up in Gaz's room above the pub, making their own entertainment. Normally Michael was well up for some home entertainment after a breakup, and he wasn't sure why he was so dead against it now, cos Christ, wouldn't a bit of something uncomplicated be just what he needed? But somehow it felt *wrong*. And the more he tried to think it through, tried to work out what was going on in his head, the more wrong it felt. And the more sad.

But he couldn't stay in and watch telly with Mum, because he just *couldn't*, all right? So he ended up going for a run, going miles further than he usually did, probably setting a new personal best for speed, as if that fucking mattered to *anyone*. He staggered home sweaty and exhausted to find Mum asleep in front of *Question Time*, all those sodding politicians arguing with each other, yap yap yap, shouting and ranting and saying sod all that was any use to anyone.

Michael hauled himself upstairs and had a bath, then towelled himself off, flopped on the bed, and lay there staring at the ceiling.

How come he'd never realised how empty his life was?

It'd seemed fine before he'd met Rufus, and Christ, just thinking about him set off a wave of longing that hurt like fuck. Shit. Maybe he should bite that bloody bullet and say something to Mum? Whatever happened, it couldn't feel worse than this, could it?

He didn't know. He just didn't fucking know.

Michael closed his eyes for a long moment. Then he pulled on some jogging bottoms and went downstairs to wake Mum up so she could go to bed.

CHAPTER 19
TRIP

Liz's "as soon as I can" turned out to mean "the day after tomorrow," which Rufus wasn't at all sure he was actually ready for. Despite the fact he'd moped so much the previous day that Dad and Shelley kept giving each other anxious glances whenever he walked into the room.

Shouldn't he give Michael more time to cool off? Then again, judging from past experience, that'd only make it more likely he'd find someone else before Rufus got a chance to explain things. And, yeah, ask him what *really* happened with Trix, but Rufus had to keep reminding himself about that one. Because Michael wasn't a prick, no matter what Liz thought.

"Are you sure about this?" Rufus asked for like the umpteenth time as he drove them to the ferry. They were going over Brading Down, the whole of Sandown laid out below them on the left like a really big screen showing Google Earth, and on the right, he could see across the Solent to the mainland, where Michael was. A weak winter sun kept poking its head around the clouds, making the surface of the sea all sparkly.

"Well, yeah. I'm not letting you face this on your own."

"I mean, leaving Kieran all day? With Shelley?"

"He loves his Auntie Shelley."

"Yeah, but— *Shelley*? Aren't you worried she'll, I dunno, forget to feed him or leave him on a bus somewhere?" Oh god. Should he have left her the car after all?

"Roo, if your stepmum was mentally incompetent, I don't think your dad would have married her. She'll be fine. She's babysat for me before."

"Not for a whole day."

"She'll be *fine*. Look, we're doing this, all right? So stop being like the merchant of gloom. You're giving me a headache."

Rufus fell silent, and tried to enjoy the drive. Which was hard, cos now the best bit was behind them and they were onto the main roads, or at least what passed for main roads on the island. Rufus had never driven on the mainland, but he'd heard it was a lot different, with, like, multiple lanes and traffic systems *everywhere*.

And if he was really, brutally honest with himself, worrying about Kieran had been a bit of a welcome distraction. Now he wasn't worrying about that, all kinds of other worries were creeping in, like maybe Michael would just slam the door in his face. Or Trix would never give them the address. Worse, they'd get to Trix's place only to find she and Michael had got back together . . .

And then there was the other thing.

Rufus drove past Queen Victoria's old country cottage and through East Cowes to the ferry terminal, where they got directed to lane three, and parked behind a Peugeot with two enormous black dogs in the back. Their ears pricked up as he pulled on the handbrake, and they gazed at him, panting, their tongues hanging out like they were really happy to see Meals on Wheels had just delivered.

"Boat's in," Liz said, pointing as if somehow Rufus might have managed to miss a bloody great car ferry. Although to be fair, most of it was hidden around the corner, behind some boxy red brick buildings. There didn't seem to be a lot of people travelling today, which on a weekday in early March wasn't all that surprising. There were more trucks than cars, most of them belonging to supermarkets.

Rufus stared, wide-eyed, as a thought hit. "Oh my god, I just realised. If there's a zombie apocalypse, the Isle of Wight's going to starve, isn't it? Cos, yeah, they could stop the ferries running and maybe the people would be safe from the virus or whatever, but no *way* is there going to be enough food to go round."

"Nope. I give it a month before people turn cannibal. A week if it's summer and we've got all the grocks here too."

Rufus shuddered, remembering a couple of guests at the B&B who'd *not* been happy when they'd run out of sausages for breakfast one morning. "Couple of days, I reckon. Um. Are you sure this is a good idea?"

"Jesus, don't start *that* again!"

"It's just . . ." Rufus clenched and unclenched his hands on the steering wheel. "What if there's, you know, an accident or something? Or I get on the ferry and I'm not all right? I mean, they're not going to bung it in reverse and come back, are they?"

Liz twisted right round in her seat to give him a hard stare. "I thought your ferry thing wasn't a real thing?" she said slowly.

Rufus took a deep breath, his hands all clammy on the wheel. "It's. Um. It's a bit of a thing."

"Rufus! You told me it wasn't."

"I never said it wasn't a thing."

"You told me it was all about your mum. When she was ill. Your dad made you go on this school trip to see some play, and when you got on the ferry you threw a wobbly—"

"Had a *panic attack*."

"—cos you were worried she was gonna die while you were off the island. And then you made out like it was all about worrying the boat was gonna sink, cos you didn't want your mum to know why it really happened."

"Well, yeah. Basically."

"And ever since then you've been using it as an excuse every time your dad goes all noble and says you oughtta get off the island and train as a chef, cos you're worried Shelley'll leave him if you're not there to do all the work in the B&B."

"Pretty much."

"Roo, have you ever stopped to think there is *so much wrong* with all this? You know your dad wants what's best for *you*, not for him. *And* I don't reckon you're giving Shelley enough credit, either."

Rufus stared guiltily at his worryingly white knuckles. "She doesn't know anything about running a B&B. You know that."

"Maybe if you lot—that's you *and* your dad—stopped treating her like a total airhead, she'd stop acting like one?" She glared at the dogs in the car in front. One of them let out a mournful howl, and both of them lay down and stopped looking out the window. "Anyway, this is *so* not the point." Her voice softened. "Roo, your mum died years ago.

Your dad's fine. You haven't *really* got a thing about boats, so why are you getting in a flap about this one?"

"I don't know, all right? It's just . . . I was fifteen. How do I know what I was really panicking about? What if it *is* a thing? What if I really *am* gonna have to stay on the island all my life?"

Liz's face was set to *does not compute*. "Well, wouldn't you wanna know?"

"No! Not if the answer's bad. I mean, yeah, I want to stay and help Dad, but . . . what if that's the only thing I *can* do? It'd be, like, the Isle of Wight's turned into Alcatraz."

"That's bollocks. There's always other things you can do. Like hire a helicopter."

"Yeah, and pay for it with what? My *soul*? How am I going to manage that, every time I want to pop home to see Dad and Shelley?"

"Look, this isn't the point. The point is, if you never try and get on a ferry, you're gonna be stuck here all your life anyway."

"But I won't know I'm stuck."

"Yes, you will. Cos I'm gonna call you up every day and tell you 'You're stuck,' until you grow some balls and get on this fucking ferry."

"Why are you so keen to do this anyway? You don't even *like* Michael."

"Cos it's not about Michael, this. Have you even been *listening*? It's about you, confronting your thing." Liz sniggered. "And if you're really lucky, at the end of it all you get to confront Michael's thing."

"Har har."

"Now come on, the bloke's waving at you. Time to man up and get on that boat."

Rufus took another deep breath, and followed the black dogs to his doom.

"Well, that was a bit of an anticlimax," Liz said half an hour into the ferry crossing, shoving a chip in her mouth.

Rufus glanced up from his plate. "Hey, we're only halfway across. I might still panic."

"Yeah, and I *might* agree to go out with that bloke in the caff who was eyeing me up, but no one round here's holding their breath."

"Fair point. Have you got any more ketchup left?"

Liz rummaged through the pile of sauce sachets she'd picked up. "Nope. Brown sauce, mayo, or vinegar."

"Mayo, please. Ta." Rufus squeezed it onto the edge of his plate and dunked a chip thoughtfully. "You know, I thought it'd be like being on the train or a bus or something, but it's more like waiting for a train in the station cafe. If I didn't know we were moving, I *really* wouldn't know we were moving."

"Yep. Welcome to the thrilling experience of being bored off your tits on the Isle of Wight ferry. But you must've been on it before—I mean, before the one with the panic attack."

"Yeah, but . . ." Rufus screwed up his face, trying to remember. "Far as I remember, it all seemed a lot more exciting, then. Cos, well, I hardly ever went away with the family, what with the B&B. And school trips are different, cos you're with your mates." He beamed. "Hey, I'll be able to go and visit them now." Most of his old mates had moved off the island when they finished school, and only ever came back at Christmas and the summer holidays. If their parents had moved off, they never came back at all.

"See? *This* is why I wanted you to do this." Liz waved her chip around in emphasis. "You're free now. You can do anything you want." Her eyes turned sly. "Do any*one* you want."

"Michael's the only one I want," Rufus said, and glared at her. "So we are *not* turning round and getting on the next ferry back home, yeah? We're going to find him."

"Yeah, whatevs. You got a pen? Someone's left a *Daily Mail* on the table over there, and I wanna do the puzzles."

CHAPTER 20
FALL

rix's address was in Calmore, which was out of Southampton on Salisbury Road and would've been dead easy to find even if Rufus hadn't had GPS on his phone. It was just as well. Mainland roads really were different, and Rufus was getting tired of other drivers honking their horns at him. He was doing his best, all right? It wasn't his fault he kept getting in the wrong lane.

As it happened, he could tell how close they were getting by the way the butterflies in his stomach kept multiplying. "How do we even know she's going to be in?" he fretted, hunched over the wheel. "It's Friday, right? She might be working."

"They took a week off, remember? So there's a fair chance she's there. And if she's not, we just camp out on her doorstep until she gets home, okay? Right—it's over there, yeah?" She pointed, and Rufus pulled into the small parking area that luckily had several vacant spaces. He parked next to someone's Jeep and hoped the Focus wouldn't get a complex about it.

Trix's building was one of those modern, red-brick blocks of flats that weren't at all blocky and had windows where you'd least expect them. There was a security door at the bottom, with buttons to push for the individual flats so you could try to persuade the occupants it was safe to let you in, even though the speaker thing made you sound like a Dalek. Luckily, though, someone had propped it open with a brick, so they just went straight on up the stairs to flat three's front door.

Liz paused, her fist inches from the door. "Right, here we go. And Roo? Leave all the talking to me, right? The last thing we need is you going all gooey-eyed over her bastard ex."

"Yeah, yeah, I know the drill."

"Well, don't forget it. I know what you're like. You're totally useless when you're in *lurve*." She rapped sharply on the door.

There was a wait of about a minute, which was just enough time for Rufus to start thinking, *Oh god, she's here but she's in bed with Michael, they're totally back together, shag, shag, shag*, when it opened.

"Yeah?"

Rufus stared. The woman in front of them was, like, *enormous*.

And not in a cuddly, curvy-girl way. She was about seven feet tall—all right, maybe not, but she met Rufus's gaze without either of them risking a cricked neck—and had the arms and shoulders to go with it too, nicely showcased in her muscle tank top.

Worse, her hands were all wrapped up in those bandages boxers wore under their gloves.

Rufus swallowed. "Um . . ."

"Hi, I'm Liz!" Rufus *did* crick his neck then, whipping his head around to stare at his best mate, who'd bounded forward with a breathy cry and a manic smile. "You must be Trix!"

Trix gave Liz a cautious smile. "Yeah, that's right. Have we met?"

"No, of course not! I'd have remembered!" Liz giggled. There was even the suspicion of a snort.

Rufus gaped at her, struck so dumb he thought he'd probably never speak again. Had she gone *insane*? "We're friends of Judy's, at the Selsey Hotel," he said quickly, before Liz could get even more worrying. Okay, so he'd been wrong about never speaking again.

"Oh, yeah?" Trix's tone was a different sort of cautious from before.

Rufus glanced at Liz, but she was still doing that weird thing with her face. And her hands.

And her entire body.

Wonderful. Looked like he was on his own here. "Yeah," he answered. "She said, like, you had a bad experience with a bloke there? Michael O'Grady," he clarified, although there was a fair chance Trix hadn't forgotten him.

Her face darkened. "What's he to you?" Her nostrils flared.

Rufus stepped back a pace, worried she was about to start pawing the ground. "Um, he, well . . ." Drying up, he elbowed Liz in the side. Hard.

"Ow! Yeah, that's right. He totally did."

Trix frowned. "Did what?"

"Um, hurt Rufus. Yeah. Like a bastard." Liz nodded manically.

"So we wanted to get revenge, yeah?" Rufus threw in. "'Cept we don't know where he lives."

Trix paused, then nodded. "Okay. He's at 23—"

"We need to write that down!" Liz burst out with. "Can we come in and borrow a pen?"

Rufus frowned. "I've got one."

"No, you haven't!"

Rufus and Trix both stared at Liz.

"Yes, I have," Rufus said slowly. "Remember? We were doing the puzzles on the ferry with it."

Liz's eyes darted wildly. "Then I borrowed it. And dropped it overboard. Remember?"

She trod on Rufus's foot.

Really, *really* hard.

Trix snorted a laugh. "Yeah, why not? Come in, Liz. You and your . . . boyfriend?"

"Oh, Rufus isn't my boyfriend!" Liz giggled again, stepping into the flat. "We're both, like, totally gay!"

The giggling was bad enough, but Rufus *really* wished she'd stop talking in exclamation marks.

"Yeah? That's great," Trix said, leading them into a small living room mostly occupied by a large punchbag hanging from a bracket on the ceiling. Oh god. She looked like *she* was about to start giggling any minute.

Rufus wanted to run far, far away.

"I'll put the kettle on, yeah?" Trix said, leaving them in the tiny living room, staring at the punchbag. She moved to a pocket-sized kitchen area and started to unwrap her hands, which hopefully meant she wasn't planning on punching anything soon.

Liz grabbed Rufus's arm. "Oh God. Kill me now. Did you *see* her?"

"She's a bit hard to miss," Rufus whispered back.

"She's *amazing*. And I'm making a total *tit* of myself. I am, aren't I? Oh God."

"Yep. At least a double D. Maybe even a double E. You *like* her?" Rufus hoped Trix hadn't overheard the disbelief in his voice.

She might decide she needed a new punchbag.

"Are you blind?" Liz whispered *way* too loud. "She's, like, an Amazon or something. But with two boobs. Oh God, did you see her boobs?"

"Not particularly." He'd been too busy looking at her shoulders. And feeling totally inadequate in comparison. The knowledge Michael had come straight from her bed to his, via a minor detour into Sandown Bay, wasn't helping either.

"Tea, yeah?" Trix called from the kitchen area. "How do you want it?"

"White, ta, no sugar," Rufus called back.

Liz didn't say anything, so he elbowed her. "Ow! Just white, please!"

"Like her women," Rufus's inner demon couldn't help adding.

"Ignore him!" Liz squeaked. "That is so not true! Um. Not that there's anything wrong with being white. I like white girls. I'm white myself. My kid's half-white." She buried her head in Rufus's shoulder. "Oh God, you bastard, kill me *now.*"

"How did you and Clea ever manage to get together and produce Kieran?" Rufus muttered, amazed. "Were you, like, struck dumb that day or something?"

Liz muttered something into his sweater that sounded a lot like "laryngitis."

"Sit down, yeah?" Trix said coming back with the mugs of tea, all hostess-like.

She was *so* not what Rufus had been expecting. He and Liz sat on the squishy leather sofa, and Trix perched on a chair opposite. "How old's your kid?" she asked.

"Twenty-seven months," Liz said, managing to sound a bit more normal. "Been potty-trained for nearly three months now," she added proudly.

Trix leaned forward. "You gotta give me some tips on that. My sister's kid's nearly three and still in nappies, and it's driving her mental."

"Well, see, the key thing is—"

Rufus coughed loudly. "Um. Michael's address?"

Liz glared at him.

Trix looked a bit uneasy. "Look, I had a chance to think about it while I was making drinks, and I'm not sure I oughtta tell you where he lives. See, I dunno what he done to you, but I was thinking, he's got this thing? Like, you get all taken in by the smile and stuff, and you think, 'Yeah, he's the one'? But, like, it doesn't mean as much to him. And that's not his fault, see? That's just the way he is. And when you're *not* with him, you start thinking, oh my God, what was I *thinking*? Like, I went way overboard on him when he dumped me. Like, *way* overboard."

Rufus nodded fervently, although there was a weird feeling coiling inside him like an animated Chelsea bun, laced with the cinnamon of doubt and lightly sprinkled with the icing sugar of unease. *Had* he just been a bit of fun to Michael after all?

"So maybe right now you're thinking, what a total bastard, and you wanna go round and egg his house or kick his lights in or something, but maybe if you left it a couple of days, you'd feel different?"

"I won't feel different!" Rufus burst out with.

"Yeah, but still—I mean, he's not my best mate or anything, and I'm still gonna kick the shit out of him next time I see him—" She must have seen something in Rufus's face. Or Liz's face. Or both of them, cos she caught herself. "Kickboxing, yeah? We go to the same club."

"That is so awesome," Liz breathed.

"Anyway, so I'm not sure I oughtta give you his address. Sorry."

Rufus stood up, sloshing tea on his jeans. "But you've got to! And, ow."

"What've you got planned for when you find him?"

"Um ..." Rufus crumbled. "Look, I just want to talk to him, okay? He left cos of something he thought about me, and it wasn't true."

Trix's big brown eyes went all soft and wet, like dates soaked in brandy. "Look, din't I just tell you, he's got this thing? You'll get over him. I mean, how long have you known him? Couple of days?"

Well, yeah. Technically speaking. But they'd been a really *intense* couple of days. "Sort of?"

"Well, there you have it. I'd known him for weeks, and I got over him."

"Yeah, but . . ." But it was different for Rufus, because him and Michael had been *real*, yeah? But no way could he say that.

"I mean, God, I even proposed to him." Trix laughed. "God, what was I *on*?"

See, this was where he'd expect Liz to shove her oar in and say, *Yeah, why did you do that?* But she was still all gooey-eyed and giggly. Rufus sighed. "Why did you do that?"

For the first time, Trix went a bit pink. "Look, I'd been having a rough time, yeah? Family and all that shit. See, my brother Harry, who's two years younger than me, he rang last week to say he's got his wife up the spout *again*. And my brother Hayden, who's *four* years younger than me, he's getting hitched to his girlfriend Kaycee in the summer. 'Cept they don't want me to be a bridesmaid, cos I'm 'too tall and it'd put the photos all out of balance,' but anyway, they're sure I wouldn't wanna do it cos I never wear dresses. And yeah, maybe I don't, but I could've made an exception. Or even worn the same as the ushers, couldn't I?"

Liz nodded, rapt.

"So anyway," Trix carried on. "I'd been feeling a bit crap and left out, all right? And then I met Michael at kickboxing, and he was great, know what I mean? Din't treat me like a girl when we sparred, and when we went out, he was all over me like a turbo-powered octopus on Viagra. It was flattering, all right? Sort of thing that makes a girl feel special. And he never gave me the sleazy crap I get from most guys, who—*if* they're not too shit-scared of my height or my muscles to go out with me in the first place—always seem to think 'I'm bi' is code for 'I'm just gagging to act out all your stupid lesbian porn fantasies for you to wank off to.'" She paused for breath. "And there was this bloke on breakfast telly in the morning, going on about it being the traditional day for girls to propose to their blokes. And *then* I get this text from Hayden, the wanker, who must've seen it too, telling me the big three-oh's coming next year, like I don't *know*, and the twenty-ninth of Feb could be my last chance to not get left on the shelf."

"You realise that's, like, a totally outdated patriarchal concept that degrades women, yeah?" Liz said dreamily.

"Well, *yeah*," Trix said, leaning towards her. "I just wasn't thinking straight."

"And it's total bollocks saying a girl can't propose any day she bloody well wants to, yeah?"

"I know, all right? I just lost my head. It's so hard, innit? When you got your family on your back with all this 'time to settle down' crap and 'I only want you to be happy.'"

"God, I hate that one," Liz said, nodding. "Like, 'you'd be so pretty if you grew your hair long.'"

"Or, 'you only go out with girls who look like men, so why don't you just stick to men anyway?'"

"God, yeah. They got no idea, have they?"

"Not a clue."

Rufus coughed so loudly he hurt his throat. "Um, excuse me? Can we get back to the point, here?"

They turned to him with identical looks of surprise, as if to say, *Oh, are you still here? Why?*

Teeth-grinding, Rufus reminded himself, was a really bad habit and he didn't want to get into it. "Michael's address, please?"

"Oh, that," Trix said. "He lives in Redbridge—you know, just down the road from here? Number 23, Coronation Road. But seriously, you don't wanna go there. He's a self-centred bastard, and his mum's a total witch. Like, no one's ever gonna be good enough for her precious baby boy."

"I knew it," Liz put in. "Bet she spoiled him rotten when he was a kid. My Kieran's gonna be brought up proper. There'll be none of this entitled bullshit from him."

"Good for you. I bet he's really cute, your kid. You got a picture?"

"I've got, like, zillions on my phone. Hang on a mo." Liz rummaged around in her backpack. "Here you go—that's Kieran on the swings yesterday."

Trix came over to sit close to her on the sofa. *Very* close. "Oh my God, he's *adorbs*! He looks just like you too."

"Wait a minute, I'll find the one with him all dressed up like a tiger for his second birthday . . . There you go. Is that cute or what?"

"Oh my God, I could just *eat* him!"

"And wait till you see him blowing out his little candles—I got that on video—"

Rufus had seen that video more times than he'd cooked hot dinners, and all right, it was totes adorbs, but enough was enough. He stood up, stumbled into the punchbag, and righted it hurriedly before it could swing back and knock him over. "Right, time to see Michael."

Liz didn't move.

"Um, aren't you coming?" he asked after a mo.

"You don't want me cramping your style," Liz said immediately. "And anyway, you should, like, leave me here as security."

"Security? What for?"

"Uh . . . In case we've been lying to Trix, and you really are just out to slash Michael's tyres and chuck bricks through his windows? I mean, she's only got our word for all this."

Trix nodded, shifting closer to Liz on the sofa, which Rufus hadn't thought was actually possible. "Yeah. You stay here, right, and when your mate comes back from Michael's, we'll take him out for lunch to cheer him up."

"Good idea," Liz said. "You got any good pizza places round here? He always likes pizza when he's moping, don't you, Roo? And ice cream, that's good too."

"Who says I'm going to need cheering up?"

They both turned to give him sad little smiles. "Nobody," Liz said reassuringly.

"Yeah, course not," Trix agreed with about the same level of sincerity as a politician come polling time.

Somehow that was *worse*.

The short drive from Calmore to Redbridge seemed to happen in some kind of weird wibbly-wobbly timey-wimey thing, where it felt like it took forever but was still somehow over *way* before Rufus was ready for it to be. The houses on Coronation Road were arranged in short, identical terraces of four houses, with the odd semi thrown in here and there to confuse you, and Michael's house was one of the middle ones in one of the middle terraces. Unlike most of its neighbours, it still had a front lawn and hadn't converted it to off-road parking. There was a Saab convertible parked outside, looking a bit lonely.

Most of the street's residents were out at work and had taken their cars with them, Rufus supposed. At any rate, it made it easy enough for Rufus to park Dad's Focus only a hop, skip, and a jump away.

Not that Rufus felt much like hopping right now. Or skipping and jumping, for that matter. He was pretty certain, the way his legs were shaking, he'd just end up falling flat on his face. Now he was here, this whole trip seemed a bit, well, stalkerish. Maybe what happened on the island should have stayed on the island?

Would Michael even want to see him?

He knocked, and waited.

The door opened.

And Rufus found himself staring straight into Michael's wide, blue eyes.

Rufus dredged up a wobbly smile. "Surprise," he said.

Michael wasn't smiling. Although he did look surprised. "Fucking *hell*."

CHAPTER 21
BARGE

Michael stared. What the hell was Rufus doing here? Not on the island. On the mainland. *Here.* At Michael's house.

At his *mum's* house. Michael's chest was tight. It was like some bastard had just hosed him down with cold water, which was doing its best to freeze him to the core.

Come to think of it, it was a lot like the first time they'd met. Christ, he was gonna go insane.

"W-what?" he stuttered, which was at least better than "fucking hell," although not by much.

"Um," Rufus said. "So the ferry thing? Not so much a thing. Long story. Can I come in and tell it to you?"

Michael's mouth unfroze a bit quicker than the rest of him. "No."

Rufus's face fell.

"Michael, who is it?" Mum called out from the kitchen.

Shit. "Jehovah's Witnesses," he yelled back. Mum hated them worse than she hated buy-sex-you-alls. "Look, you can't come in," he whispered urgently to Rufus.

"Oh." Rufus blinked several times. "Right. Okay." He swallowed and turned away.

Shit.

Shit, shit, *shit.* "Look, I don't want you to go, but it's my mum, yeah?"

"Your mum?"

Shit. Michael glanced back into the hallway, then stepped outside, pulling the door to behind him. "I'm not out to her, all right?"

Finally he got it. "Oh. Oh my god. Sorry. Um. I'll, um . . ." Rufus looked at him as if Michael would have the first idea what to do now.

Christ, this was a mess.

"Look, there's a pub down the road, yeah? The Pig and Whistle."

"You want me to meet you there?"

"No!" People *knew* him in there. People who might talk to Mum. "But you turn left after the pub, carry on down the road, and there's a bit of parkland, right? Meet you down there in ten minutes." He stepped back inside and closed the door in Rufus's face, a trickle of cold sweat running down his spine and into his crack. Shit, that was gross. And itchy. And Jesus fucking Christ, what the hell? Rufus had been the *last* person he'd expected to see here.

Christ, his hands were shaking. He couldn't believe Rufus had just turned up out of the blue. What about his bloody thalassophobia, which hadn't been on Michael's word-of-the-day calendar but he'd looked it up on the internet, all right? Michael fought the urge to open the front door again to check Rufus really had come here. He'd probably legged it by now, anyway.

Oh God.

Michael needed to get down the road right now, before Rufus got fed up waiting and buggered off again. Shit, he'd be there, wouldn't he? He wouldn't just shove a finger up in Michael's general direction and get back on the ferry, would he? Not after coming all this way, facing his ferry thing—although he'd said it wasn't a thing, hadn't he? Michael was well confused.

"Michael?" Mum hobbled into the hallway. "Oh, you've got rid of them. Good. I've told you before, you don't want to get talking to these people. You can't reason with them."

"Mum, I gotta go out."

"You'll be back for tea?"

"Yeah. Definitely. See you later, yeah?" Michael grabbed his jacket and jammed his feet into his trainers. Then he ran down the road towards the scrappy bit of park he'd told Rufus to meet him at, telling himself Rufus would *be* there, all right? Why wouldn't he be?

Then again, why *would* he be? Some evil bastard kept whispering nasty little things in Michael's head. Like, *You didn't exactly roll out the red carpet, did you?*

Oh God. But what the hell was he supposed to *do?* Michael sped up. He'd thought he might pass Rufus on the way, but there was no sign of him. Did that mean he hadn't come this way? Michael's heart was pounding when he rounded the corner into the park—and saw Rufus standing under a tree, hugging himself.

Thank God.

"Oi, Rufus," he called out. Rufus looked up but didn't come to meet him. Michael jogged up to the tree. "You all right?"

He didn't smile. "Yeah, fine. Bit chilly, though. Like the welcome."

Christ, stab him in the heart, why not? Michael swallowed. "Uh, yeah, sorry about that."

"You never told me you weren't out to your mum," Rufus said accusingly.

Michael felt he was entitled to get a bit narked about that. "Oi, I never knew you were gonna turn up at our house without a word of warning, did I? Last *I* heard, you never left the Isle of Wight."

"I *tried* ringing you, but your phone's never on. What was I supposed to do?" The words were bolshie, but Rufus just looked sad. He blinked a few times. It was making Michael feel weird inside. Like he wanted to hold him and stroke him and keep him safe. Preferably while punching something.

"You never let me explain about the ferry thing," Rufus went on. "You just stormed out in a huff. *And* without explaining about Trix."

"Yeah, like anyone was gonna believe my side of the story." Michael's need to punch something was getting stronger. That tree they were standing under had better watch its fucking step.

"I'd have believed it!" Rufus gave him a challenging look. "So tell me now, all right?"

Shit. "Look, I didn't know she was gonna propose, yeah? I'd only known her a few weeks. I mean, come on. If I'd known that was what the holiday was all about, I'd of run a bloody mile before I got on a ferry with her. For fuck's sake, we'd seen each other literally three or four times. Who the bloody hell wants to get *married* after that?"

"It could happen," Rufus insisted. Then his eyes narrowed. "Even if she *does* now realise she had a narrow escape."

"Maybe she does. I ain't seen her." Michael shrugged. "Not in that much of a hurry to put myself in the firing line. Anyhow, you've heard my story. Gonna believe it?"

Michael looked Rufus right in the eye and folded his arms to show it was no skin off his nose either way. Except his guts felt like someone was filming a remake of *The Birds* inside him, and that bastard trickle of sweat was back and itching like fuck. "Well? I ain't got all day."

Rufus met his gaze steadily. "I believe you. But . . . does it even matter?"

What the fuck? Michael took a step forward, then stopped, his fists clenched by his sides and his fingers itching to grab hold of Rufus. "Does it *matter*?"

"To you, I mean." The breeze blew a few strands of blond hair over Rufus's eyes. He didn't seem to notice. "Do you even care what I think? Do you care about *me*? I mean, it's all right if you don't. You've only known me a couple of days. Probably less hours added up than you and Trix spent together. But I just . . . I need to know. That's all."

Michael's insides melted. And his outsides. He was just one bloody big puddle on the ground. He barely had the strength to close the gap between them and grab Rufus so fucking tight they were gonna turn into some weird composite freak thing out of a horror movie. "I care, all right?"

Shit. It was *true*. Michael was still reeling from the realisation when Rufus kissed him.

Christ, he'd missed this. It was like . . . like he'd been chugging along on standby, and Rufus had just flicked the On switch. Michael felt like he was glowing, like some stupid fucking sparkly vampire or a shed-load of toxic waste. It was like when you got in a hot shower after a winter's run, and you hadn't even noticed how cold you were until you got warm again. He *needed* Rufus, yeah, like food or air or all that sort of crap. He needed him like water. Water . . .

Still keeping firm hold of Rufus, cos like he was letting him go ever again, Michael broke the kiss and pulled back to give Rufus a searching look. "So what's the story with you and water, then?"

"What? Oh, you mean my ferry thing? Um. It's sort of a bit, um, made up. I mean, originally it was so's not to upset Mum when she was ill, but then Dad kept saying I should go and do an apprenticeship in a London restaurant, and him and Shelley would be fine without me, which is, like, *so* not true. So I thought if they thought I couldn't leave the island, they'd get off my back about it and not feel guilty."

That was just Rufus all over. Thoughtful, self-sacrificing, and kind of complicated. Fuck, Michael lov—was into him. "So what do they think about you being here today?"

"Um. They think I'm on Tennyson Down, looking at the Needles."

Michael laughed. "What are you, some kind of rebel? Seriously, when are you gonna get your act together and get your own place? Preferably this side of the Solent, cos I don't think there's a mile-high club for ferries."

"You know I can't do that. Dad needs me in the B&B."

"No, he doesn't. You're not even taking bookings right now."

"We will be soon. And there's always stuff that needs doing. We can't decorate the guest bedrooms when there's people sleeping in them, can we?"

Shit. "So how were you thinking this was gonna work? It's no good me going over to yours, with your dad trying to keep us six feet apart all the bloody time."

"He'll come round. And why can't we go to your house? You can just say I'm a friend. You know, until you're ready to tell your mum about us."

Michael looked at Rufus. Really *looked* at him, with his delicate features, his earring, and the little rainbow pin in his jacket, which was just the cherry on the . . . the . . . Fuck it. Michael didn't even *like* cherries, stupid things, more stone than fruit and how the hell was anyone supposed to be able to do the tongue thing with the stalks anyhow? "There's no way on *earth* Mum's gonna believe you're a mate of mine." Even if by some miracle she did believe it, she'd be nagging Michael to ditch him as a bad moral influence.

"So why not just tell her about us?"

Michael stared into the sky. "I *can't*, all right? I can't be gay."

"I'm not asking you to be gay. You're bi, right? So what's wrong with that? Your mum loves you, doesn't she?"

Course his mum loved him, but . . . "You don't understand. She's old-fashioned, and she's dead religious. She's not gonna go for it. Look, we can still see each other, right? We'll just have to be a bit careful."

"For how long?"

"I dunno, do I?" Christ, way to put him on the spot. "We'll see how it goes, yeah?"

"What, so we'll just keep meeting in deserted parks and stuff? And lying to your mum? That's dead romantic, that is."

"So what, you're getting all fucking goody-two-shoes about sneaking around behind my mum's back, but you're not gonna tell *your* mum and dad you're able to leave the island?"

"That's different! It's for their own good."

"Oh, and keeping Mum happy's just me being a total selfish bastard, right?"

"You really think she wants you to keep her happy by denying who you really are?"

"I'm not denying nothing! I'm just keeping quiet about it, that's all."

"That's the same thing! Look, I know what it's like, coming out. I was worried before I told Mum and Dad I was gay. But it's something you've just got to man up and do."

"Why? Seriously, why?"

"Cos a twenty-six-year-old man who's still scared of what his mum thinks is seriously not sexy. And I'm not sneaking around and helping you lie to her."

"But lying to your own parents and sneaking off the island is just fine, yeah?"

"I . . . Fine." Rufus folded his arms. "I'll tell them, all right? *If* you tell her. Agreed? Cos if not, I'm going home right now and that's it."

That bastard with the hose and the ice-cold water was at it again. Michael felt like if someone hit him now, he'd shatter.

It wasn't fucking *fair*. "I can't, all right? I just can't."

Then he turned and walked away.

CHAPTER 22
RICOCHET

Rufus was amazed he didn't have an accident driving back to Trix's, cos his eyes were all blurry and he was having a *lot* of trouble concentrating on the route. It wasn't fair. He'd come all this way. Faced his (all right, not particularly existent) ferry fears. He'd even agreed to come clean to Dad and Shelley, which was going to have consequences *way* beyond what Michael thought.

And Michael wouldn't even come out to his mum?

Rufus parked the Focus any-old-how in front of Trix's flat and trudged up the stairs to bang his head gently on the door.

When Trix opened it, he almost fell flat on his face.

"How'd it go?" Liz demanded.

Rufus sniffled. "Pizza?" he begged plaintively.

"Oh, Roo-roo." She came to give him a hug. Strong arms wrapping around him from the other side indicated he was the sausage in a girl-on-girl sandwich.

Michael would probably really enjoy this, Rufus thought with a pang of sadness.

"I told you he was a shit, din't I?" Trix said soothingly. "You're better off without him. Like me, yeah?"

"Yeah," Liz agreed. "So go on, what happened? Do we need to go round there and sort him out for you? Did he, like, slam the door on you? Tell you to piss off?"

"He said he wanted me to be his secret boyfriend. I mean, I even said I'd tell Dad I haven't really got a phobia, and he still—"

"Wait a minute, you what? I don't believe you. I've been on at you for like *five years* to tell him the truth—"

"You've only known me four years."

"—and all he has to do is gaze at you with his big, brown eyes—"

"They're blue."

"I don't care if they're fucking polka-dot. Jeez, will you stop interrupting?" She glared at him. "What was I talking about?"

"Does it matter?" Rufus burst out with. "There's no point now, is there? I'm not going to be his dirty little secret, and he's not going to come out to his mum."

Trix frowned. "Well . . . Have you met his mum? I mean, I told you she's a witch, din't I, babe?" She glanced at Liz, who gave her a gooey-eyed smile.

"'Babe'?" Rufus asked. "Since when are you 'babe'?"

"You were gone a long time," Liz said defensively.

"Not *that* long." Rufus sniffed. "Just long enough for my heart to be broken and all my dreams shattered," he added bravely.

"Yeah, see? Takes time, that sort of stuff. Oh, fuck off, don't look at me like that. I know you liked him, but it's not like he's the love of your life. How could he be, when you've only known him a few days?"

"Sometimes you just know," Rufus told her. "It's love. You wouldn't understand."

Liz stuck up her middle finger at him.

"How do you know it's love, not just, you know, like what I felt about him?" Trix asked.

Rufus had a moment of doubt, then rallied. "Cos you had all this family pressure, yeah? Pushing you to settle down with a bloke. So, right, if you and Michael had stayed together, it would've made things easier for you. But for me, it's all the other way. I mean, my life was a *lot* simpler before I met him."

Liz gave him a pitying look. "No, it wasn't. All he's done is made you pull your head out of your arse."

"Well, it *felt* simpler."

"What does it feel like now?" Trix asked.

"Like shit. With shit on top."

"That'll be because your head's back up your arse again."

Trix butted in. "So are you gonna go and be a chef? Liz said you're amazing with food and you're, like, sacrificing your dream for your family."

Rufus heaved a whole-body sigh. "No point now, is there?"
Liz turned to Trix. "You see what I have to deal with?"

A few hours and several pizzas later, after Trix and Liz had said a
tearful farewell and promised to Skype, like, *every night*, they were on
their way back to the island. Rufus drove into the ferry terminal and
handed his ticket to the woman in the little booth. She tore it in half,
just like his heart, and directed him to lane five.

"Hang about," Liz said slowly just as he was setting off again. "Isn't
that Shit-bag over there by the pier?"

Rufus twisted around and stared. Michael was there, leaning
against the door of his Saab with his arms folded. He had a pissed-off
expression on his face.

Rufus had never seen anything more beautiful. He slammed on
the brakes, then hit reverse. A car coming into the terminal swerved
just in time and went into the other lane, horn tooting. Rufus didn't
care. He zoomed up to Michael, parked the Focus next to the Saab,
and almost fell out of the driver's door in his haste. "Michael?"

"All right. You win. You want me to tell my mum you're my bloke?
Fine. Get in."

"What?"

"Get in. We're going there now."

Dazed, Rufus got into the Saab. He was vaguely aware of Liz
shouting something from the Focus, but it probably wasn't important.
"We're going to tell her?"

"Yep." Michael turned the key in the ignition, and the Saab roared
into life.

"And . . . you want to be my boyfriend?"

"Looks like it, don't it?" Michael pulled out onto the road. "But
you'd better fucking well not have been joking about holding up your
end of the bargain."

Rufus's insides were doing a happy dance. If he hadn't been
strapped into the car, the rest of him would have been following suit.
Nothing, not even gruffly voiced ultimatums, could burst his bubble.
"So we're going out, yeah? Properly?"

"Yeah."

"Like boyfriends?"

Michael swallowed. "Yeah."

"And you're going to tell *everyone*?"

"Don't push it." Michael glanced over. "Fine, yeah, I'll tell people. If they ask. I'm not taking out a sodding ad in the papers."

That was all right. Rufus could Facebook it anyway. "This is amazing. What changed your mind?"

There was a silence.

"Michael?"

"I just . . . I like being with you. Don't want to never see you again. You make me wanna *do* stuff, like, good stuff, you know? You make me think about stuff that's not just getting laid and having a good time. And you made me feel like a fucking coward, you bastard. Telling me to man up, *Christ*." He huffed, hands tightening on the steering wheel for a mo. "But yeah, I thought . . . Maybe it's time I told Mum about me and blokes. Like you said, leap years are for trying something new, yeah?"

Rufus's heart broke all over again, then melted into a big, gooey puddle on the floor of the Saab, where it oozed lovingly around the empty Mars Bar wrappers and condom packets. "Oh my god. That's, like, the nicest thing anyone's ever said to me."

"Yeah? You need to get out more," Michael muttered, his cheeks pink and his eyes fixed on the road.

"If you weren't driving, I'd totally jump on you right now."

"Yeah, well, no jumping on me when we get there, right? I wanna break this to Mum gently, not by acting out a bloody porno in her front room."

The rest of the journey passed in a happy glow. The sun was low in the sky, turning all the colours richer and bathing everything with optimism. Rufus couldn't believe he'd gone from despair to delirium so quickly. Michael liked him. He really, really liked him.

Even Michael's house, when they got there, had a rosier hue than when Rufus had last seen it. The front door, formerly so stern and unwelcoming, now seemed to beckon him in.

Michael paused, his key in the lock. "Look, just remember she's really religious, yeah? So don't expect her to be all happy about you and me being . . . you know."

Bless. Rufus gave him a reassuring smile. "It'll be fine. People's mums always seem to like me."

"Christ, I hope you're right." Michael took a deep breath and opened the door. "Mum?"

A lady about Dad's age hobbled into the hallway, drying her hands on a tea towel. She looked tired, a bit drab, and like she had too many aches and pains for her age. And she seriously needed to get her roots done, poor love. They showed white for a full inch at the parting of her dark brown hair. Shelley would've been horrified.

"Mum? This is Rufus. I met him on the island, yeah?"

Rufus smiled at her.

"Oh?" Michael's mum gave him a very searching look. She didn't smile back. "Nice to meet you, Rufus. Are you just passing through here?"

Rufus looked at Michael. Michael swallowed, his Adam's apple bobbing under its sexy coat of stubble. Then he spoke. "Nah. We're sort of going out, me and Rufus."

"Going where?" Her tone was a bit sharper than Rufus would've liked.

"Not going somewhere. Going out. He's my, um, my b-boyfriend." Michael's face had gone a worrying shade of pea green.

His mum's lips tightened. "Michael, would you come into the kitchen, please?"

Michael paled to the colour of baby leeks. "Right."

They disappeared, leaving Rufus to examine himself nervously in the mirror by the door. The crucifix on the wall behind him loomed over his shoulder in silent reproof, which was just as well, as any audible reproof would have been drowned out by the furious argument going on in the next room. It was a bit embarrassing. No, scratch that. It was a lot embarrassing. And hurtful. And horrible. Rufus could hear every word. And the word was *no*.

"Michael O'Grady, I don't believe what I'm hearing. A *boy*friend? Have you taken leave of your senses?"

"Mum, can't we just sit down with a cup of tea and you can get to know him, yeah?"

"No, Michael. I'm not having him here. Not under my roof. It's not right."

"But Mum—"

"No. You may tell me that who you choose to go around with is none of my business, and maybe you're right, for all I'm your mother. But bringing that . . . boy here is *making* it my business. And I'm not having it. What would your father say?"

"How the bloody hell do I know? I never met him!"

"And I'll thank you not to speak of him in that tone of voice. He'll be spinning in his grave." There was a sound halfway between a sniff and a sob, and when she spoke again, her voice was so soft Rufus could barely hear it. "Lord knows I've tried to bring you up properly. It's been so hard. A boy needs his father."

"Mum, this has got nothing to do with Dad, all right? Look, just come and meet him properly, yeah?"

"I will not. It's that girl, isn't it? Trix. Putting immoral ideas in your head."

"This is nothing to do with Trix! I've always liked blokes as well as girls."

"But you don't have to *act* on it. How could you, Michael? When you know perfectly well how I feel about this?"

The tortured figure of Jesus on his wall-mounted cross gazed reproachfully down at Rufus. He seemed to be saying, *What do you expect from a worshipper of Poseidon?* Rufus felt horrible. Gut-wrenchingly, miserably horrible. He'd forced Michael into this.

It was just . . . He'd thought it would go *well*. That Michael's mum would say, *Bless, I always knew you were a bit light in the loafers*, which was pretty much what Rufus's dad had told *him*. Or, worst-case scenario, she'd have brief conniptions, burst into tears, and then be all *Whatever makes you happy, dear*. That'd been Granny Robins.

How could he have been so *stupid*? So quick to be all *whatevs* about Michael's worries, because it wasn't like he might actually know his mum's views on this sort of stuff, oh no, he'd only known her *twenty-six years*.

Rufus was the actual dictionary definition of a stupid, selfish, deluded, home-wrecking, prickish *arse*.

One thing was certain. He couldn't stay here.

His heart breaking into, like, a million pieces, he walked out of Michael's house.

Out of Michael's life.

CHAPTER 23
PLUNGE

Michael heard the front door open and close, but ignored it. Rufus wasn't gonna get far. Michael had the Saab's keys in his pocket. Mum was going on about *men* and their *urges*, and how they were the devil's work and you just had to think pure thoughts till they went away. Like it was all just about his dick, for Christ's sake. As if he'd have brought Rufus to meet her if *that* had been all it was.

"Mum, you don't get it. Rufus is . . . It's not just sex, all right?" Why couldn't she see that?

"I know what it is, Michael O'Grady. I know *just* what it is, and thank the Lord, it won't last."

Ouch. That kneed him right in the balls, that did. And what did she even know about it anyway? She'd barely spoken to Rufus. "What the hell is it, then, eh? Go on, tell me. What would you call it?"

"Well, it's certainly not *love*."

"Because he's a bloke?"

"Of course because he's a man! What kind of *love* is it that causes you to throw over a perfectly nice young woman—"

"Mum, you hated Trix."

"—for a young man with the loosest of morals?"

"I met Rufus *after* me and Trix split up, all right? It was nothing to do with him. And you know *nothing* about his morals." Michael flushed, his conscience kicking him in the teeth. All right, so they'd shagged the first time they'd met. Didn't mean it hadn't *meant* something.

Eventually.

Look, she didn't sodding well know about that anyway, right? So who was she to judge?

Mum put her hands on her hips. "And you've known him, what? All of three days?"

"Yeah, but . . . I've never felt like this about anyone, okay? It's scary. He makes me wanna be better." Michael swallowed. His insides felt raw, just coming out with it like that.

But it was the truth. *That* was why he was doing this, why he was finally, after all these years, making a stand against his mum's old-fashioned attitudes. Because he couldn't stand Rufus thinking he was a fucking coward—and worse, knowing it was true.

Mum wasn't impressed. "Better? *Better*? By going against God's law? And who's *he* to say there's anything wrong with you the way you are?"

Christ, she just didn't *get* it. "He doesn't. He's never said anything like that. It's just . . . he's not scared of who he is, and he's always doing stuff for people. He's great, Mum. Say one of the girls wasn't married and she brought someone like him home, you'd *love* him. Admit it."

"I'll admit no such thing."

"That's just cos you haven't had a chance to get to know him. Haven't *given* him a chance."

"I know *quite* enough about that young man from what you've told me of him. I certainly don't want to know any more. And what do you suppose Father Thomas would say if he were here now?"

"What the bloody hell's it got to do with him?"

"What about Our Lord, then? What do you think He'd have to say about you . . . *fornicating* with a young man?"

"Mum, this is the twenty-first century, not five hundred BC or whenever Jesus was around. You were fine about me and Trix going on holiday together, and you've never got on my case when I've had girls over for the night." *Their* case, yeah. But not Michael's. "If Jesus is so concerned about my bloody sex life, why would He want me to be having it with a girl I wasn't married to, either?"

"Don't try and tell me this is the same. It's nothing like."

"It's exactly like!"

"The Bible says—"

"The Bible says a lot of shi—*stuff* we never bother about. Why is the bit about blokes loving blokes so much more important than the rest?"

"Because it's disgusting!"

It echoed through the room, ripples dying away into the awful silence.

When he'd been around fourteen, yeah, Michael and his best mate, Col, had nicked a couple of six-packs of Col's dad's beer and got wasted. He'd come home reeling, swearing, and stinking of alcohol.

Mum had slapped him round the face. Hard. Even through the drunken haze, it'd hurt like fuck. Not the slap. The fact she'd done it to *him*.

It'd been years before he dared to drink again.

This . . . this felt worse. It felt like she'd hollowed him out with a spoon, like Col's mum had used to do to pumpkins before carving a face on 'em at Halloween. "Me and Rufus, yeah?" he heard himself saying, 'cept it didn't sound a lot like his voice. "You think we're disgusting?"

"I most certainly do, and I won't have it. Not in my house." Her face was stone.

"Right. Fine. Guess you won't want me living round here any longer, then."

Michael blinked once, and headed up to his room, ignoring the shouts of "Michael O'Grady, you get back down here this instant!" His bag was still packed with all the stuff Rufus had washed for him. That'd do him for a bit. He picked up his work phone and chucked it in. Then he shouldered the bag and went back downstairs.

Mum was standing in the hallway, not an inch of give in her expression. "And just where do you think you're going?" she demanded.

"Dunno. But I'm going there with Rufus," he said, forcing himself to look her in the eye. Well, near enough. In the face, definitely.

She'd cave now, right? Tell him if Rufus meant so much to him, then she'd come round to it. Tell him she loved him too much to lose him over this.

Right?

Mum's lips tightened. "If you leave this house now, Michael O'Grady, don't you even *think* of coming back."

"I'm sorry, Mum. I gotta." Michael stepped out of the house he'd grown up in, feeling like someone had just ripped his whole skin off and left him raw and bleeding. He'd never . . . He'd never thought

Mum would speak to him like that. Not *him*. He'd always been her favourite. Even his sisters just treated it like a fact of life.

Although now he came to think about it, Faith had seemed sort of bitter at Christmas when she'd said something like, "Well, of course she's going to leave *you* the house."

Huh. Not looking so likely now.

Where the fuck was he gonna go? Thinking about it, Michael didn't reckon any of his sisters'd turn him away—well, maybe Faith— and he had plenty of mates who'd let him kip on their sofas. But they were all straight. He just wasn't sure how happy any of 'em'd be if he turned up with a boyfriend in tow.

Christ. A boyfriend. Michael swallowed. He was still having a bit of trouble with that word. Maybe if he thought of it as "a Rufus" instead?

Yeah. He could cope with having a Rufus. That'd do for now. There'd be plenty of time to get comfortable with using the b-word.

Maybe he could go to Col's? They'd shared enough mutual wank sessions in the past. Or Gaz's? They'd done pretty much *everything*.

Michael snorted. Yeah, right. He could just see himself explaining that one to Rufus.

Which brought up another problem.

Where the *fuck* was Rufus?

Shit. Michael slung his bag in the back of the Saab and drove off up the road to look for him, the setting sun in his eyes making them water.

And yeah, it was definitely the sun, all right?

Shut up.

CHAPTER 24
HURTLE

Rufus wandered down Coronation Road in a haze of pain. His shadow stretched out yards in front of him like a grim portent of his future. He needed comfort. He needed his mu— No. He needed Liz. Grabbing his phone, he hit Call.

Liz answered almost immediately. "You *arse*."

This was not quite as comforting as he'd hoped. "What have I done?"

"Only abandoned me at the ferry terminal with a car I'm not insured to drive. *Arse*."

Oops. "But you got on the ferry, right?"

"How could I? I'd have had to get another ticket to travel on my own. How far do you think my benefits *go*? And I wasn't gonna leave you here on your own with that shit-bag."

"Michael's not a shit-bag. *I'm* the shit-bag."

"What's that supposed to mean?"

"I made him come out to his mum. And she's, like, *totally* against it. Didn't even want me in the house."

"So where are you?"

"Halfway down his road now."

"So . . . let me get this straight. You told him he had to come out to his mum or you'd leave him? So he told her. And you left him anyway. You're right. You are a shit-bag."

Oh fuck. She was right. "But I did it for him! He's better off without me."

"Hear that *clip-clop* sound? That means it's *way* too late to shut the stable door now. And while we're on the subject, how come you get to choose what's best for everyone? Might wanna work on that god complex, just saying."

"But what do I *do*? I can't just go back there. That's not going to make his mum like me any better."

"Hang on a mo." There was a pause, filled with the muffled sounds of a conversation Rufus couldn't quite hear. "Right. We're gonna pick you up."

"Who's 'we'?"

"Me and Trix. I called her, din't I? After you buggered off and left me. She picked me up from the ferry terminal, and we're on our way back now. We're gonna swing by and get you."

"But what about Michael?"

"I dunno, do I? I can't solve *all* your problems for you."

"I can't . . . I've got to go back." Even if Michael's mum called him *that boy* again in a tone that made it sound like she'd rather her son was shagging a cockroach than Rufus.

"Jeez, make your mind up. Look, we're nearly there anyhow. We'll see you in five minutes, yeah?"

"Um. Yeah?" Rufus hung up, not much caring if they came or not. Whatever happened, he wasn't going anywhere until he'd spoken to Michael again. And explained he hadn't *meant* to be a shit-bag. Rufus turned and ran back the way he'd come, blinking into the last of the sunshine.

Of course, deciding he had to talk to Michael was easy. Getting up the balls to actually knock on his door was, like, planetary orders of magnitude more difficult. There seemed to be some weird gravitational effect on his feet that made them much, much heavier the closer he got. By the time he managed to reach the door and raise a fist to knock on it, it was like he was moving in slo-mo. He kind of expected the knock to come out as a big, echo-y boom, but no, it was just his normal hesitant rap.

Michael's mum opened the door. In tears. When she saw it was him, she let out an actual sob.

Rufus felt like a total selfish bastard. "Oh my god, I'm, like, so sorry. This is all my fault. I thought you'd be okay with it, yeah? And that's why I told Michael I didn't want him to lie to you about us. I just didn't *think*. Is Michael in?"

She shook her head mutely, a hanky pressed to her lips. Why her lips? Did she cry through her mouth? And yeah, when Rufus looked, the Saab was gone from the road outside. He'd thought the place looked different, somehow. "I am *so sorry*," he said. "He'll come back though, yeah? You know what he's like. He gets all funny if you give him an ultimatum. Just has to go away and think about it for a while. Look, why don't we go inside and I'll make you a cup of tea?"

To tell the truth, he was a little worried about her, but once he'd got her sat down in the kitchen with a nice cuppa and a choccy biccy, she got a bit more colour in her cheeks. Still hadn't said anything, mind, but that was okay cos Rufus was babbling away for England. "Is there someone I can call? One of Michael's sisters? Not the one who's expecting, cos she needs to put her feet up, poor love—one of my teachers at school had twins and she was like totally round for the last three months—but one of the others? Which do you think would be best: Faith or Hope? I always reckon hope's a good thing to have, but from what Michael says, you're probably more into faith. I was brought up Church of England, which I always think is just code for *not really sure about anything*. But in, like, a respectful manner. Um. More tea?"

She shook her head and took a deep, shuddering breath. "H-he's told you all about us, then?"

"Yeah. And about his dad, which was, like, *so sad*. I lost my mum when I was sixteen and that was pretty horrible, but at least I got to know her, you know? It must have been so hard for you."

She took a sip of tea and put the cup down, where it rattled on the saucer. Rufus had known she'd be a cup-and-saucer person, not a mug person. He could tell these things. "How old are you now, Rufus—it is Rufus?"

He nodded. "I'm twenty. Although I've just had my fifth birthday—bit of a funny story—"

"You're a leap-year baby?"

Rufus beamed. "Yes! How did you know?"

She actually smiled. Well, a bit. Sort of. "Michael's father was a leap-year baby. My Michael. He used to joke about me being a cradle snatcher, a girl of eighteen carrying on with a boy who hadn't yet had his fifth birthday."

Yeah, jokes like that were probably funnier in those days. "That's amazing," Rufus said. "I mean, you'd think, statistically speaking, there must be loads of us leaplings, but I *never* meet any." Of course, for the last four years or so he hadn't really got out much. "You must've married really young," he added, nudging the plate of biscuits closer to her.

"Eighteen, I was, and Michael not much older. I never even looked at another man. I don't think it's right," she said, and Rufus was queasily certain she wasn't talking about having a roving eye. Her next sentence confirmed it. "You can't tell me it's natural for two men to . . . be together. You say you're Church of England?"

Rufus nodded, sending a guilty mental *sorry* to Poseidon, who hopefully wouldn't turn out to be the vengeful sort when it came to aposo . . . apost . . . people who changed their religion. Rufus still had at least one more ferry crossing to survive.

"Well, then. Do you really think such a life is what Our Lord would want for you?"

"Well, the way I see it, Jesus was all about love, yeah? So I don't think He'd mind a bit more love in the world." Rufus was actually fairly confident on that one, cos he'd heard it from a gay vicar he'd snogged once. Probably best not to mention that to Mrs. O'Grady, though.

She gave him a sharp look. "And that's what you'd call it, is it? Love?"

Rufus could feel his cheeks going pink. "Um. Sort of? I mean, okay, we haven't known each other all that long, but look at me, yeah? Off the island for the first time since my mum died. I wouldn't do that for just *anyone*. But please don't tell him I said that. It might make him feel all ultimatum-y again."

"I'm sure you'll be seeing him before I do." She took another sip of her tea and closed her eyes for so long, Rufus started to wonder if she'd fallen asleep. Then she startled him by standing up, her eyes wide open and a determined look on her face. "When you see Michael, tell him . . . tell him I didn't mean what I said. Tell him to come home."

Um. That meant it was time for Rufus to go, didn't it? He stood up too, and carried the cups over to the sink. "Are you sure you're going to be all right?"

She nodded. "I'm going to call my daughter now. You—travel safely."

It sounded a bit grudging, but the thought was what counted. "Thank you. And I'll tell Michael what you said."

If, he thought as he closed the front door behind him, he ever managed to find Michael again.

Funnily enough, that turned out to not be too hard.

All he had to do was follow the shouting.

Rufus jogged down the road to where the noise was coming from, which was where Michael's Saab and Trix's Jeep were pulled in at the side of the road, having a face-off. Michael, Liz, and Trix were standing by their cars, having a shout-off. With added bonnet-thumping.

Yikes. Michael and Trix were kickboxers, weren't they? Rufus hoped Liz would have the sense to keep out of it. Although the closer he came, the more it looked like it was Liz yelling at Michael, and Trix was the one keeping out of it. Rufus wondered what they were fighting about. Okay, yeah, he'd known there was a fair bit of mutual hostility, but he'd thought it was on a low simmer, not boiling over into what looked like imminent violence.

"What the hell have you done with him?" Liz screamed.

Michael was dark-faced and dangerous looking, which Rufus should *not* have found so attractive. "Me? Don't you try and game me—"

"Hello?" Rufus said nervously.

"Roo!" Liz flung herself on him so hard it actually hurt. She was small but solid. And bony.

Michael glared at them. "Christ, where the hell have you *been*, you tosser?"

"Um, with your mum."

Everyone stared at Rufus. It was like one of those dreams he still had occasionally, where he turned up to school completely naked and thought he'd managed to hide it until Mr. Blackmore (it was always Mr. Blackmore, who'd reeked of pipe smoke, liked to stand too close when correcting Rufus's work, and had a disturbing way of rolling the *R* at the start of his name) asked him to go up to the front, and everyone pointed and laughed.

"With *Mum*?"

"Yeah, we had a cup of tea and a biccy. She said she didn't mean it and she wants you to go home." There. Duty done.

"Mum . . . let you in the house?"

"Well, I sort of let myself in. I mean, she obviously needed looking after."

Michael just carried on staring at him. It was a bit unnerving, and was making Rufus's eyes want to water in sympathy.

Liz gave an exaggerated *tut.* "It's what he does. Give her your recipe for sticky toffee pudding, Roo, and she'll love you forever. Right. All sorted. Now can we *please* get back to the ferry before they stop running them for the night and my little boy has to cry himself to sleep thinking his mum's abandoned him?"

"Liz, it's only just past his teatime. And I need to talk to Michael, okay?"

"I'm coming with you," Michael said out of nowhere.

CHAPTER 25
CLEAR

"**Y**ou're coming with us? To the ferry terminal, or to the island?" Rufus looked surprised, fuck knew why.

"The island. At least for tonight." Because Michael needed somewhere to stay anyhow, and fuck if he was letting Rufus out of his sight again. At least until he was feeling a bit less shaky.

"What about your mum?"

That stabbed him right in the heart. "I can't go back there. Not tonight. I'll ring her, all right?" Michael added quickly as Rufus started to frown. "She . . . said stuff, yeah? Need a bit of time to get my head round it."

"Oh. *Oh.*" Rufus flung his arms around Michael, which was great, was more than great, was just what he'd needed, *Christ*—if it hadn't been for the tiny, panicked voice inside him going, *Oh fuck, this is the street where you live, everyone will see, they'll know you're a poof, oh fuck oh fuck oh fuck.*

Michael told his inner coward to fuck off and die in a fire. He'd have told it to take his inner homophobe with it too, 'cept he had a nasty feeling they still had some unfinished business to deal with.

He was getting there, all right?

"I didn't mean to leave you," Rufus was saying into Michael's neck. "I just thought you'd be better off if I wasn't there."

"Yeah, yeah," Liz said impatiently. "Noble and self-sacrificing, blah blah blah, Jesus, you're worse than your dad. Who, by the way, you're gonna be having a serious conversation with before the week's out. Come on, we've got a ferry to catch."

"You gonna be all right going in a car with this tosser, babe?" Trix said.

Michael frowned. "Trix?"

"Not you, you tosser. I'm talking to Liz."

"Oi, since when is *she* 'babe'?" Not that Michael cared, but trying to work out what was going on was giving him a headache. "And who are you calling a tosser?"

"You, you tosser." Trix did the hand gesture as well. "Going to kickboxing next week? Better get Rufus to kiss your balls good-bye first, cos I'll be ripping 'em off to hang 'em from my rear-view mirror. Tosser."

"Yeah? You and whose army?" Michael grinned, glad she didn't seem to have too many hard feelings about it all. "Now we're not going out together, I won't have to worry about holding back when we spar."

"Holding back? You wish. Liz, babe, you take care, right? And if that tosser gives you or Rufus any shit, you tell me. I know how to deal with him." She bent down to give Liz a sloppy kiss, then straightened to give Michael the finger.

Michael shook his head. *Lesbians.*

Shit. Did he just say that out loud?

It'd explain why Trix was suddenly right up in his face. "I'm bi, remember? Despite all your attempts to put me off men for life. And what's your problem with lesbians, anyway?"

Michael backed off a step and held up his hands, with a bit of difficulty as he still had Rufus hanging round his neck like the world's most fuckable fashion accessory. "Nothing. I got no problem with lesbians. Just thought you're living the stereotype a bit, that's all. You know, like the joke? 'What does a lesbian bring to a second date? A U-Haul.'"

Trix folded her arms, her eyes narrowed. "You wanna talk stereotypes? How about the bi bloke who shags anything that holds still long enough, eh? I've heard *all* kinds of stories about you, screwing around like an alley cat what's never had the snip. People like *you*"— she jabbed a finger in Michael's direction. Michael swung Rufus out of the way just in time to avoid him getting a nasty stab wound in the back from her fingernail—"are what give people like *me* a bad name. I've had it up to my tits with blokes thinking 'bi' means 'total slapper.'"

"Oi, can you stop bad-mouthing me in front of my bloke? That's all in the past, yeah? I'm with Rufus now." He stroked Rufus's hair, smiling at the way Rufus snuggled in closer. He half expected him to start purring like Charity's cat. Although hopefully when Rufus had had enough petting, *he* wouldn't try to take Michael's arm off.

When Michael looked up, Trix and Liz were both staring at him, open-mouthed.

"What?" he demanded, annoyed.

"That was actually . . . sort of romantic," Liz said at last. "Are you sure you're gonna be all right to drive? Not feeling feverish, delusional, any of that kind of crap?"

"Fuck off."

Liz rolled her eyes. "No, he's fine," she said, turning to Trix. "Later, yeah? Make sure your internet connection's stable, cos you're not gonna want to miss a *second* of what I've got planned for tonight's show. And you," she added, spinning back to face Michael. "Don't even *think* about perving off on the thought of me and her getting it on, right?"

Huh. That hadn't even occurred to Michael.

Christ. He really did have it bad for Rufus.

Rufus lifted his head, leaving Michael's neck and shoulder feeling sad and cold. "You and Trix can totally perv on the thought of me and Michael getting it on, though. We don't mind."

Michael nodded, cos it was a fair point and he could afford to be generous.

Trix made a face, and Liz said, "Thanks, we'll pass."

They were only jealous, because, face it, who *wouldn't* wanna perv on the thought of him and Rufus together? "So are we getting this ferry or what?" Michael asked.

"We're getting this ferry," Rufus said, and kissed him.

Michael didn't *think* anyone he knew was around to see it.

Care. He meant, he didn't *care* if anyone he knew was around to see it.

Definitely.

The girls had one last snog, and Liz climbed into the Saab's back seat, where she started bitching about the lack of leg room. Michael ignored her and drove off, one hand on Rufus's thigh. He'd meant it about not letting him go again.

They had sausage and chips on the ferry, although Rufus and Liz didn't seem all that hungry and just picked at theirs. And then Michael got thinking about what'd just happened with him coming out to Mum and stuff, and then *he* lost his appetite, and they all just sat there staring at full plates of overpriced food going cold.

Michael turned to look at Rufus, which was a definite improvement on chips going soggy and sausages cementing themselves to the plates with their own grease. "I know why I'm not hungry, but what's your problem?"

Rufus bit his lip. "I think I ate my body weight in pizza earlier. And ice cream. Plus, well, I've got to tell Dad about my ferry thing, haven't I?"

Fuck it. Michael put his arm around Rufus's shoulders. "Look, you don't have to, just cos I—"

"Don't you dare," Liz cut him off. "He's telling him. And if you don't"—she turned to Rufus—"*I* will, all right? It's for your own good," she added smugly. "Time you started living your own life, not your dad's."

"Yeah, your dad's doing all right for himself, ain't he?" Christ. Michael was agreeing with Liz about something. His world really had turned upside down today. "Him with his young bit of fluff and all. How'd that even happen, anyhow?"

"What, Dad and Shelley? She came to stay the summer before I met Liz. Booked a room at the B&B for a fortnight, and never left. Think she was a bit lonely," Rufus added, looking thoughtful. "It was her first holiday since her first marriage broke up, and she was all on her own. So she didn't really go out much in the evenings, and they got talking. A lot."

"Was he an older bloke and all? Her first husband?"

"Bit, I think. She never really talks about him much. Although she did say once that he left her cos she couldn't have kids, which is a totally bastard thing to do."

"She can't have kids?" Liz leaned forward over the table. If her boobs had been bigger, she'd have been dunking them in her ketchup. Michael sniggered under his breath at the thought. "You never told me that."

"It never came up. Well, actually, she told me not to tell anyone. Oops. She probably only really meant Dad, though."

"Why? Your dad doesn't want any more kids, does he?"

"Don't think he minds either way. But I think she feels embarrassed about it. Like it's a failing or something." Rufus made a face. "Think her first husband was a bit of a shit about it, actually."

"And they couldn't have tried to adopt?"

"Don't think he wanted anyone else's kid."

"Tosser." Michael stretched, and peered out the window. He felt sorry for Shelley, yeah, but he didn't wanna talk about mums and kids right now, all right? "We nearly there yet?"

Liz's lip curled up. "You're all heart, you are."

CHAPTER 26
RATTLE

Rufus drove back home with just Liz as a passenger, as Michael had brought his car on the ferry rather than leave it parked at the terminal. It meant the journey was a bit more peaceful than it might otherwise have been, but Rufus was still obscurely relieved to see the Saab parked in front of the B&B when they pulled up in the Focus.

"Thought how you're gonna explain this to the folks?" Liz asked as they got out.

"Um. Not really. Maybe a sort of good-news-bad-news thing?"

"As in, the good news is, you got on a ferry and left the island, but the bad news is, you picked up something nasty while you were over there? Pun totally intended."

"I'm right here," Michael said. He didn't sound *too* narked though, so Rufus ignored him.

"Hey, Michael's the *good* news." Rufus worried at his lip with his teeth as they walked round to the side door. "Well, he will be once I've explained things properly."

He opened the door, to find Dad, Shelley, and little Kieran sitting around the kitchen table, finger-painting. "Mummy, mummy, mummy!" Kieran shouted, jumping down to toddle over to Liz and leave paint-smears all over her jeans.

"How's my darling little man?" she cooed, picking him up and holding him at arm's length. "Have we been painting? Have we been using washable paints this time, or does Mummy have to have words with Auntie Shelley and Uncle Gerald again?"

Dad beamed up at them, then obviously caught sight of Michael. He frowned and opened his mouth.

"I went on a ferry!" Rufus said quickly.

"Really? That's wonderful," Dad said, standing up. He had one blue hand and one green one. Luckily, unlike Kieran, he wasn't really the hugging sort. "And you didn't have any problems?"

"Nope. Must be cured," Rufus said, crossing his fingers behind his back and his toes inside his trainers for good measure.

Shelley got up too. Her hands were yellow and red. Rufus backed off a step. "Yeah? That's great, love. I'm really pleased for you." Her smile looked a bit wobbly, though. "S'pose the world's your oyster, now. You won't want to be hanging around here with us old folks." She walked over to the kitchen sink and stood there for a moment, looking perplexed, until Rufus realised what the problem was and turned on the taps for her. "Cheers, love," she said, rinsing her fingers. "Not that it's not lovely to see him," she added, "but how come your Michael's here?"

"*Is* he still your Michael?" Dad asked, his frown deepening.

"Yeah, so, it turns out Judy got the story a bit wrong, yeah? Or, well, not *wrong* exactly, but—"

"Jesus, save me from you trying to talk me up," Michael interrupted him.

Dad put his hands on his hips. Rufus winced for his cardigan, now adorned with primary-coloured handprints. "Well, if you'd like to explain yourself . . .?"

Michael looked like he'd rather jump straight back into Sandown Bay.

Rufus had to intervene. "He came out to his mum for me. And she chucked him out the house."

"She never!" Shelley put a thankfully clean hand to her mouth. "Her own son?"

"Her *only* son," Rufus clarified, laying it on with a trowel but so what? "Course, she chucked me out first."

"Oi," Michael butted in. "She didn't chuck me out. I just told her if she was gonna make me choose, then I was gonna choose Rufus. And anyway, it's not her fault, yeah? She's religious."

Which was, like, the *best* thing he could have said, cos while Rufus was going all melty about it, Dad softened right up too. "Sit down," he said, pulling out a chair for Michael. "Rufus?"

Rufus knew his cue. "I'll put the kettle on."

"And I'm off home," Liz announced. She'd somehow managed to clean Kieran up in the meantime, bundle him into his coat, and shoulder the bag with all his stuff. It was like she had magical mum powers.

"On your own?" Michael asked gruffly. He looked a bit embarrassed by all the attention.

"Yeah, it's not far," Liz said blithely.

He stared her down. "It's dark. I'll walk you. What? You think I'm giving Trix *another* reason to kick the shi—stuff out of me?"

She rolled her eyes. "Fine, whatever. Make yourself useful, then, and carry the bag."

He grabbed it, and they left.

Rufus filled the kettle, set it on to boil, then sat down at the kitchen table. The finger paintings were quite pretty, although Shelley's was definitely the best, all smiley faces and sunshine. Kieran had gone for a more abstract approach, and Dad had tried to do animals but they hadn't really worked. Rufus wasn't sure exactly which animals Dad had tried to portray, but speaking personally, he would definitely have gone for an even number of legs. Then again, was that just him being ableist?

Something was itching at the back of Rufus's neck, and he looked up to find himself the subject of a couple of heavy stares. "What?"

Dad coughed. "Ah, Michael?"

"Um, would you believe he's a total sweetie when you get to know him? Oh, and I met the ex, and she's, like, totally no hard feelings about it all. Well, maybe *some* hard feelings, but she's actually really glad he turned her down." Rufus paused. "Um, this still isn't making Michael look good, is it?"

"Rufus, love, you know your dad and me just want you to be happy. Don't we, love?" Shelley glanced over at Dad, who nodded hastily.

"Absolutely." Then he frowned again. "But why didn't you tell us you were going to try a ferry trip?"

"Um, I didn't want you to be disappointed if it didn't work out? But anyway," Rufus added quickly. "You know I'm going to stay here, right? I mean, I'm not going to leave the island now, just cos I *can*."

Dad and Shelley had a quick exchange of glances that left Rufus wondering (a) exactly what they were saying and (b) whether there was some kind of course married couples went on to teach them how to communicate without the kids catching on. Also, (c) if these courses were available to unmarried couples and (d) gay ones in particular, cos it'd be really useful if he wanted to, say, arrange a shag with Michael without Dad and Shelley catching on. Then again, (e) was it just the one language that everyone learned, which would make it a bit useless in this particular instance?

Rufus was just getting to (f), which was going to be something really profound about whether teen slang had evolved as a direct reaction to (b), when the door opened and Michael walked back in.

Michael levelled his gaze at Dad. "Right. No need to get a room ready. I'm gonna be bunking with Rufus."

"Is that so?" Dad asked in a sort of mildly interested voice that managed to subtly convey that anything that was gonna happen would happen with his approval or not at all. "Rufus?"

"Um, kettle's boiled, who's for tea?" Rufus sprang up from the table and started clattering around with mugs.

He probably missed whole *conversations* going on silently behind his back. Which was a definite bonus.

Michael coughed behind him. "Gonna take my bag up," he said gruffly.

"Oh, okay," Rufus said without looking up. He was a bit busy juggling tea bags.

There was a short silence, broken only by Michael's footsteps.

"Um, love?" Shelley said hesitantly. "Think you might wanna..."

Rufus looked round. Dad gave him a gentle smile. "I think your young man might be a little upset after the way things went with his mother. Why don't you go up to him, and I'll make the tea?"

"Oh. Oh, right." Rufus put down the mug he was holding. "Um, Dad? You're not mad at me for bringing him back here?"

"No. Now, off you go."

Rufus took a deep breath and hurried up to his room.

Michael was sitting on the bed, looking lost. He glanced up from his contemplation of the duvet cover. "Liz said she's gonna come over tomorrow. Said she's got a couple of ideas."

Rufus blinked. "Ideas? About what?"

Michael shrugged. "Din't say."

He looked back down at the duvet, which honestly didn't rate all this attention. It was a plain old boring abstract pattern in blues and greens. Rufus's Killer Baker duvet cover with the skull and crossed whisks was *way* more interesting.

Rufus sat down next to Michael and snuggled up. "She'll come round. I mean, she's already come halfway round. Well, at least a third. And she said she didn't mean what she said, whatever it was."

Michael nodded. "Yeah. It's just . . . she's my mum, you know?"

"Yeah." Rufus bit his lip. "I'm really sorry. I should've listened when you said she'd have a problem with it."

"'S okay. I shoulda told her years ago. It's just . . . she's always been on my side, yeah? I didn't want her to . . . not be. I shoulda said stuff, though. Told her she was wrong, all that stuff she used to say about gay people, not let her think I felt the same way she did." Michael looked up. "'M glad you left when you did. Wouldn't of wanted you to hear what she said."

Rufus wondered what he meant. "Your mum? She seemed, you know, nice. I mean, apart from the homophobia."

"Yeah. Got it in one." Michael gave him a twisted smile. "S'pose we oughtta go downstairs again, yeah? Don't want your dad thinking we're getting up to stuff in here."

"Don't care," Rufus said firmly. "I've been thinking. I mean, they know now I'm staying here to help run the B&B cos it's my choice, not cos I'm stuck on the island. So it ought to be on the basis I'm an adult, and I get to do what I want with who I want, in my own room. Um. Although we should probably still keep the noise down, cos it'd be totally embarrassing if they heard us, or, like, knocked on the wall to complain."

"So that's what you're gonna do, is it? Stay here? Not be a chef?"

Rufus shrugged. "Haven't got much choice, have I? Can't leave Dad and Shelley in the lurch. But we'll still be able to see each other. I mean, I'll come over to the mainland lots, and you can come over here. You know you can stay here as long as you want, right? If you . . . don't want to go back home." It was probably a bit too soon to mention the moving-to-the-island plan, Rufus decided with regret.

"Might just take you up on that," Michael said gruffly. "C'mere." Michael cupped Rufus's face in his hands and kissed him.

CHAPTER 27
VAULT

Michael was still snoring when Rufus got out of bed the next morning. He felt a bit bad leaving him there on his own, but his stomach had remembered that uneaten meal of sausage and chips and was complaining about it really loudly.

Anyway, if he got up and got cooking, he could bring Michael breakfast in bed, which meant he was being a *good* boyfriend, not a bad one. He headed down to the kitchen, where he found Shelley sitting at the kitchen table with a mug of tea and the local newspaper. "Ooh, love, have you seen this week's *County Post*?"

"No, why?"

"Your Michael's in it. There you go, it's on page seven. 'Jilted Woman Takes Revenge.'"

Rufus read the article. Well, he started it. After he'd got through *When lovestruck Southampton resident Trixie Horcambe (27) took advantage of the ancient custom that allows women to propose to the man of their dreams on Leap Day, February 28, she little dreamed she'd be callously rejected by her boyfriend, Michael O'Brady (36),* he decided not to bother with the rest. "Great piece of reporting, that. Totally unbiased and one-hundred-percent accurate."

Shelley nodded. "She's a good writer, that woman. She does the agony column too. I'd never of thought he was over thirty, though, would you? I know I got no right to talk about age gaps, what with me and your dad having all them years between us, but—"

"I'm pretty sure it's a misprint," Rufus said quickly. "They got Trix's age wrong too. She's older than that."

"Is she? Poor love. Maybe that's why she got a bit desperate? Well, I'm not going to pretend it's easy, being a single woman once you're past a certain age. All the good blokes get snapped right up." She sighed. "I worry about it, sometimes."

Rufus frowned. "You're not single. You've got Dad." And she'd better remember that.

"Yeah, but . . ." Shelley put her mug down and stared into its milky depths. "One day he's gonna wake up next to me and think, 'God, she's looking a bit saggy there.' And then he's gonna realise my looks have gone and they were all I had going for me, cos let's face it, what am I good for? I can't even keep the books without you checking I haven't gone and done something daft."

Rufus stared. "What are you talking about? Dad, like, *worships* you."

"No, he don't. I mean, I know he's fond of me, but, well, he knows what I'm like. Rubbish. And when you leave home—"

"I'm not leaving home. I said that last night."

"Yeah, but your dad and me, we talked about it last night after you went up, and he wants you to go. Says he can't expect you to bury yourself here any longer. He wants you to go up to London and get an apprenticeship in one of them fancy restaurants. And I want that too, love. I really do."

Rufus wasn't entirely sure which of them she was trying to convince, there. "It doesn't matter. I'm fine staying here."

"No, you're not. You're young, love. You should go where your talent takes you." She smiled sadly. "I never had nothing I was good at, but you shouldn't waste what you got."

"There's lots of things you're good at," Rufus insisted loyally.

"Yeah? Not to put you on the spot, love, but name one."

Oh shit. "Um . . ." Rufus had never been so glad in his *life* to see the door open and Liz walk in, Kieran in her arms. "Liz! How's it going?"

"Meh." She put a struggling Kieran down, and he toddled over to his Auntie Shelley, who beamed as she hugged him and sat him on her lap. "What you up to, then?"

"Making breakfast for me and Michael. Want some?"

"Some of us had breakfast hours ago. But yeah, go on. I'll have a bacon butty, and you can bung an egg in there too if you really want to."

Rufus fluttered his eyelashes at her. "Ooh, can I? Can I really?"

"Or I could bung it somewhere else for you. Your choice. Tell you what, me and Shelley'll go and watch *Peppa Pig* with Kieran, and you can bring it through when you're ready."

Oh. Rufus tried not to be hurt at the news his best friend would rather spend time with his stepmum than with him. Then he spotted Michael standing in the doorway with only his jeans on and forgot all about Liz. Michael yawned and stretched, his arms going up to show cute little tufts of armpit hair.

Yum. "I was going to bring you breakfast in bed," Rufus said, going over to slip his arms around Michael's waist.

Michael grinned and pulled him tight. "Yeah? Do that for all the guests, do you?"

"Only the good-looking ones." Actually it tended to be the elderly and decrepit ones, or those suffering from a case of holiday tummy, but saying that probably wouldn't have gone down so well. "Bacon and eggs all right? I think we're out of black pudding, though."

"Hey, you serve it up, I'll eat it. Why'd the girls bugger off, though? They still pissed off at me?"

"No, of course not. Why should they be?"

"They're women. Do they need a reason?"

"Probably not, if they hear you saying stuff like that. You know, you're going to have to let me go if you want me to cook anything."

Michael's hands tightened on Rufus's arse. "Maybe I don't. Maybe all I want for breakfast is your—"

"Good morning, boys," Dad said mildly, coming in with his newspaper. He sat down at the kitchen table and opened it up noisily. "Don't mind me. You just carry on."

Michael dropped Rufus's arse like a couple of buns that'd just come out of a very hot oven.

Rufus got on with the cooking. It wasn't long before he had two plates of bacon, egg, sausage, tomatoes, and mushrooms, plus Liz's bacon-and-egg butty. And Michael, who'd insisted on helping, had made almost an entire loaf's worth of toast. Which was at least half a loaf too much, but Rufus hadn't liked to tell him to stop while he was enjoying himself.

He plated up, then stuck his head round the door of the sitting room, where Liz, Shelley, and Kieran were watching cartoons. "Liz? Your second breakfast is ready."

She looked up. "So where is it, then?"

"Do you seriously want to sit there watching *Peppa Pig* while eating a bacon sandwich?"

"What Peppa don't know ain't gonna hurt her. Nah, I'll come through. You gonna be all right with him, Shelley?"

"Course I am, love."

Liz joined Rufus, Michael, and Dad at the kitchen table. Dad gave their plates a wistful look, so Rufus bunged some bacon on a slice of toast and handed it to him. Michael muttered, "Soft git," and put some of his own bacon on Rufus's plate.

Liz gave them both a hard stare. "Don't expect me to join in your little game of pass the bacon. This butty's all mine." She took a large bite, staking her claim.

"Did you check if Shelley wanted anything to eat?" Dad asked.

Rufus felt a bit guilty. "Um, no, but she doesn't usually have a cooked breakfast. Maybe I should—"

Liz *humphed*. "She's quite capable of speaking up for herself if she wants something. *Or* getting it herself."

Everyone turned to look at her.

"Um, Liz?" Rufus asked. "Want to tell us where that came from?"

"I'll tell you where it came from. It came from you treating your stepmum like she's a child, or some Barbie doll that's only there to look pretty. Maybe if you actually gave her a chance to do some stuff around the B&B, she'd do okay. Did you ever think of that? All she needs is a bit of help to get into it." Liz turned to Dad. "Did you ever, *once*, encourage her to go to evening classes or anything like that? Learn a bit about running a business? You don't let her do *anything*."

"Shelley hasn't had any experience running a B&B. It seemed—"

"She's never had any experience with kids, either, but she's great looking after Kieran."

"That's different," Dad protested. "And I gave her the books to do when she asked."

"Yeah, but we all know it's Rufus who keeps 'em straight cos she's never learned to do anything like that. Didn't it even occur to you to send her on a bookkeeping course first?"

"I suppose I thought she'd just pick it up as she went along," Dad muttered to the table.

"No, you didn't. I'll tell you what you thought. You thought, 'Drop her in at the deep end, and she'll soon see she shouldn't be worrying her pretty little head about it,' didn't you? Go on, admit it." She leaned over the table with an angry gesture of her bacon butty.

Dad drew back.

"Oi, that's not fair," Rufus put in. "Dad didn't think that. Did you, Dad?"

Dad took a moment to answer, and when he did, he sounded way more old and tired than he had a minute ago. "I just didn't want her to feel she *had* to do anything. Bad enough she's married to an old fogey like me—I wouldn't blame her for not wanting to stick around if I were to expect free labour from her as well."

Rufus couldn't listen to this. "Dad, she *likes* being married to an old—I mean, to you. She told me this morning she's worried *you're* going to leave *her*."

"Why on *earth* would I do that?" Dad's eyebrows practically hit the ceiling.

"Cos she thinks you only want her for her looks."

Dad looked completely heartbroken.

"I mean," Rufus said quickly before his insides could knot up any more from the sight, "I *told* her it wasn't just that. But she thinks she's rubbish at everything." He paused. "You know, I'm not sure her first husband was very nice to her."

"Her first husband," Liz said darkly, "oughtta be hung, drawn, quartered, and castrated. He did a right number on her self-confidence."

"I need to talk to her," Dad said, getting up.

Rufus stood up too. "We've got to tell her we think she's great. Best stepmum I could have had."

"Oi, you lot, sit down and listen to me," Liz said firmly. "We've got several problems here. One, Rufus."

"I'm not a problem," Rufus complained, sitting down.

"No, he sodding well isn't," Michael came in with supportively.

"Shut it. If I say you're a problem, you're a problem. You wanna be a proper chef, right? Which means not having time to make all the beds round here and cook everyone bacon and eggs in the morning. That's problem one. Problem two: Shelley."

"Shelley is most definitely not a problem," Dad said. He'd sat down as well, but he looked seconds away from making a dash for it.

"No, but she's *got* one. She thinks she's worth nothing cos you never let her do nothing, and she hasn't got the confidence to start."

Rufus thought he could see where this was going. "So you think I should teach her how to do stuff?"

"Did I say I'd finished talking? Zip it. No, this is where we come to problem three. Me."

Michael laughed. "Yeah, finally one we can all agree on."

"Shut it. See, I love my boy, but I'm going mental spending my whole day talking to a two-year-old. And all my benefits go on rent and kid stuff. So I want a job, but I don't wanna shove Kieran in a nursery with people who don't love him, and I can't afford to anyhow. So this is my solution, right?"

"Finally," Michael muttered.

She shot him a dark look. "One: Rufus buggers off to chef school. Piss off, do not pass Go. Two: me and Shelley do a job share."

Dad frowned. "But—"

"No buts, yeah? I'm not finished. See, it's gonna be a sort of sliding one. I did the same hospitality and catering course as Rufus, right, so I reckon I could take over what he does around here no problem. And while I'm doing that, Shelley can look after Kieran. 'Cept I'll be showing her how to do stuff as well—and maybe she can go to college and do a couple of courses, like basic bookkeeping and food hygiene and things like that—so it gets to be more and more her doing B&B stuff. I reckon by the time Kieran starts school, she'll be up to speed, so then maybe I'll look for something else, yeah?"

"Have you asked Shelley what she thinks about this?"

"Yeah, and I think it's brilliant," Shelley said, coming in with a flaked-out Kieran in her arms. "I wanna feel like I'm part of this family, Gerald. Like I'm doing my bit. And I'd love to spend more time with Kieran. And, right, I had a thought. If Liz and him lived in, she could save on rent, yeah? And if Rufus goes up to London, we'll have a room free, won't we?" She turned to Rufus. "Not that I wanna kick you out, love, of course not."

It was like driving over Brading Down, that bit where you crested the hill and suddenly you could see right over the Solent to where the whole of the mainland was spread out before you. Or, yeah, like trying for hours to launch a kite up on the cliffs, and then somehow you got it just right and the thing soared into the sky like a bird with a cat on its tail. Or like watching a really long black-and-white movie, and then when it finished, you looked around and it was like, wow, you'd forgotten there were all these colours in the world. It was like baking a soufflé—

Liz nudged him. Hard. "Oi, earth to Rufus. Wanna close that mouth before your bloke gets any disgusting ideas?"

Shelley peered at him anxiously. "You don't mind, do you? I mean, if you don't wanna go after all—"

"I want to go!" Rufus practically shouted it. "I mean, seriously, this is like the best idea *ever*. I can't believe I never thought of this before."

"I can," Liz muttered.

Rufus didn't care. "I'll be able to do my City and Guilds, get properly qualified, get trained, get a job in a place with like a million Michelin stars . . ."

"You could be the next Jamie Oliver," Shelley suggested excitedly.

Liz snorted a laugh. "Yeah, without the mockney accent, thank God."

"Or Gordon Ramsay," Shelley went on.

Dad frowned. "Well, I hope you won't let your language get as bad as *that*."

Rufus beamed at them all. This was, like, the best day of his *life*. The only thing missing right now was a celebratory snog.

He looked around, and frowned. "Where's Michael?"

CHAPTER 28
HURDLE

Michael might've known he wouldn't be able to hide from Rufus. Not that he'd tried all that hard, to be honest—just taken himself off down to the seafront to stare out at the waves. He was happy for Rufus, he really was. 'Cept . . . it was more a case of *knowing* he was happy than actually *feeling* it. He'd had to get away. Didn't wanna rain on Rufus's parade.

It was another bright winter's day, with gulls screeching themselves daft in the air and a stiff breeze whipping his hair around his face. Mum'd tell him to get it cut—

Yeah, right. *If* she ever spoke to him again. And yeah, Rufus had said she wanted him to go home, but that'd been like half an hour after the row. Less than, even. Maybe she'd had third thoughts now. And anyway, did he even wanna go home?

She'd called him and Rufus *disgusting.*

But she was his mum.

It was all seriously doing his head in, so he hopped up onto the wall, stepped over the railing, and jumped down onto the sand. It was dry as dust at this end of the beach, whipped into soft ripples by the wind and mixed in with bits of dried seaweed and old lolly sticks. The smell of the sea was so strong he could taste it, and he had a sudden memory of digging in the sand somewhere, and his mum's voice, laughter in her tone, saying, *"Look at you, Michael. You're covered in the stuff."*

His chest tight, Michael blinked—and then the spell was broken by Liz's voice yelling, "Here he is!"

He turned to see her and Rufus climbing over the railing. "Michael?" Rufus called. "Are you all right?"

He shoved his hands in his pockets. "Yeah. Guess."

Rufus gave him a look. "But?"

"Just wasn't in the mood for all that Happy Families shit."

About a dozen different expressions crossed Rufus's face, and Michael thought for a mo he was gonna apologise for being happy, which, fuck *that*. "She'll come round," Rufus said finally.

"Have you tried calling her?" That was Liz.

Michael gave her a steady look. "You planning on coming up with a solution for all my problems and all?"

"Nope. You're on your own there. But it's never gonna happen if you don't talk to her."

"Maybe it's too soon."

"No. You're her kid. It's not too soon. Trust me, I'm a mum. It probably feels like three hundred years to her."

Michael glanced at Rufus.

"Call her," Rufus said firmly. "Liz is right. She was really upset when I spoke to her."

Michael rolled his eyes. "Fine. You gonna gimme your phone?"

Just as well the landline at Mum's was the one phone number he had memorised. She'd drummed it into him when he was a nipper, just in case he ever got lost or missed a bus or anything. Michael punched it into Rufus's phone and hit Call before he had time to get cold feet.

While it rang he mouthed *Piss off* at Liz cos, jeez, give a bloke some privacy, yeah?

Rufus could hang around, though. Michael might need him, so he snagged a finger in one of Rufus's jeans belt loops and yanked so he'd get the message. Liz made a face and pissed off.

"Hello?" Mum's voice crackled down the line. It was hard to tell, but he reckoned she sounded worried.

His chest went tight. "Mum, it's me. Michael."

"Oh, Michael." No mistaking the relief there. Christ. That made two of them. Michael almost fell over with it. He hadn't realised till now just how hard he'd been braced for her not wanting to talk to him. "Are you all right? Where are you?"

"I'm on the Isle of Wight. Been staying at Rufus's folks' B&B." Michael held his breath. Maybe he'd been too quick to remind her what they'd fallen out over? But, fuck it, he was so done with hiding it.

"And you're all right?"

"I'm fine, Mum. Why wouldn't I be? You, uh, okay?" Shit. Talking to Mum had never been this hard.

"When are you coming home?"

"You want me to come home? I'm not gonna stop seeing Rufus." He wasn't gonna give her false hope, either.

"Just . . . just come home, Michael." Shit. She sounded like she was crying.

"Tomorrow, yeah? I'll come back tomorrow. Get ready for work on Monday."

"You'll be home for tea?"

"Yeah, I'll make sure I'm back by then. Look, I'd better go, this isn't my phone. I'll see you tomorrow, okay?"

"You look after yourself."

"Yeah, you too, Mum."

Michael hung up, and let out a long, shuddering breath. Then he groped blindly for Rufus, cos he'd got sand in his eyes or something and it was making them water like fuck.

Rufus held him tight and didn't say a word. Michael buried his head in Rufus's neck, breathing the scent of him in deep, wondering when home and comfort had started to smell like this. "'M going home tomorrow," he muttered. It didn't sound right. Home was where Rufus was.

"I know," Rufus said softly.

Michael raised his head. "Not gonna give you up," he said fiercely.

"I know that too." Rufus made a funny little face. "I was right here, remember?"

"'S where you belong."

Rufus nodded. "Look, I was thinking. I don't have to go up to London to be a chef. That was just a thing I thought I'd do when I was younger. But there's plenty of really good restaurants in Southampton I could train in. Or I could go to college there. Or both, you know, on a part-time thing. So I could get a room somewhere. Like, somewhere near you. Seeing as my best mate's kicking me out of house and home," he added in a louder voice, glancing over to one side. Michael followed his gaze to where Liz was talking to the old lady with the dogs from the other day.

The old lady waved. Liz sent them a sneer.

Michael felt so fucking light and happy, he could've kissed her and the old lady both. "Yeah," he said, then cleared his throat cos his voice came out a bit funny. "'Spect I'll be moving out of home soon. Think it's time, yeah? And I've got plenty of money saved up for a deposit. So, you know, I might get a place with a spare room. Or not."

"Not," Rufus said quickly. "The spare room, I mean. Definitely not."

Michael frowned. "So you're saying you don't wanna move in with me?"

"What? When did I say that? No, I mean, yeah . . . I mean, that'd be good. Moving in."

"Good." They just stood there looking at each other, grinning like a pair of idiots, until Michael couldn't take it anymore. "C'mere, you tosser," he said, pulling Rufus's face down for a kiss.

The old lady's voice quavered across to them on the thin breeze. "Are they a couple, dear? I find it so hard to tell with young people nowadays."

Liz huffed. "Yeah, they're a couple, God help 'em. I give it six months. Six weeks if they move in together."

EPILOGUE CAPER

Four Years Later

Rufus was pulling on a sweater when his phone rang. He just managed to get one arm into a sleeve and his head out of the neck-hole in time to answer before it went to voicemail.

"Happy sixth birthday, pillow-biter," Liz's voice said. "How's it going?"

He smiled into the emptiness of his old room at the B&B. "Fine, rug-muncher. And you?"

"Fine. But that is totally not true, just so's you know."

"No?"

"Nope." Liz sounded smug. "Trix waxes."

"Oh my God, I *so* did not need to know that."

"Hey, you brought up the subject. So have you heard about that job yet?"

"Well, I was going to announce it tonight, but seeing as it's you . . . Yes! You're talking to the newest chef de partie at the Fat Snail." Rufus beamed.

"Brilliant! Congratulations, Roo. I knew you could do it. It's still a stupid name, though."

"No, it's not. Why shouldn't a gastropub be named after a gastropod?"

"Cos nobody who doesn't work there or eat a dictionary for breakfast every morning actually knows what a gastropod is? So when do you start, and how soon can I have a free meal?"

"In April, and *never*. I'm not risking my new job just so you can freeload."

"Mean git. How's Shit-bag, anyway?"

Rufus did an exaggerated eye roll, which was safe cos she couldn't see it. "*Michael* is fine, thanks for asking. You'll see him tonight anyway."

"Yeah, but I was being polite. So what did his mum get you for your birthday?"

"Har har. Don't be mean. She's trying. I got cards from all his sisters and some homemade ones from the kids, though, and Faith's eldest gave me his old copy of *Stories for Six-Year-Olds*. Actually, his mum's been a lot better since she had her hip done."

"Should bloody well hope so, all those meals you cooked for her, and getting her shopping in and that. Does that mean she's come round to you carrying on with her precious baby boy?"

"Weeeeellllll . . . sort of. I mean, you know how for years, whenever I used to go round, she was always just polite, and she didn't try to throw me out or exorcise my gay demons or anything, but she wasn't exactly all *welcome to the family*? Michael always reckoned she was pretending he'd never said anything and we weren't actually together, but I thought, if that was the case, wouldn't she be wondering why he hadn't been living at home for the last few years?"

"Yeah, well, denial only goes so far. She's probably just trying not to think about it."

"But now, well, she talks to me about him almost like we're, you know, a couple. And Michael says she's the same with him too. Doesn't even mention nice girls to him anymore." Rufus paused. "They're funny, though. He *still* takes his laundry round every week, which is totally a made-up excuse to visit her. I mean, here they both are pretending he doesn't know how to use a washing machine when he repairs them for a living. It's kind of sweet." Sudden doubt assailed him. "I mean, he *must* know how to use a washing machine, right? Even if only theoretically?"

"You keep telling yourself that, Roo. So what did *he* get you for your birthday? Something pretty damn impressive, I hope. 'Specially seeing as it's your anniversary too."

"He hasn't given it to me yet." Rufus smirked. "Not the present, anyway."

"Okay, that is *definitely* TMI. Why not? Forget the date, did he?"

"Oh, he's got this plan. We're going for a walk down to the pier in a minute, and he'll give it to me then—I mean, is that romantic or what? We're going to celebrate our anniversary at the place we first met. Anyway, what time are you and Trix coming round? Shelley's locked me out of the kitchen *already*."

"Yeah, well, the menu wouldn't be a surprise if you saw the prep, would it? We'll be there around five-ish. Kieran's really looking forward to it." Kieran and Liz had moved out of the B&B six months ago and into a little house with Trix in Sandown. It was handy for Trix's job at the sports centre and for Kieran's primary school, where Liz was working as the world's coolest dinner lady.

"Yeah, so's Noah. Well, he has been since Shelley managed to convince him Kieran coming back for a visit didn't mean they were sending Noah back into care." Noah was Dad and Shelley's latest foster kid. He was four, and really sweet in a break-your-heart kind of way.

"Poor little sod."

"Yeah. Hid under the bed again. Shelley got him to come out by sitting on the floor and playing with my old toy cars for, like, ages and ages. I think they want to adopt him, but they haven't *said*."

"They're gonna put in the paperwork, but they're not sure they'll get it cos of your dad being old."

Rufus frowned. "Hang on a minute, how come you know more than I do?"

"You move off the island, sucker, you gotta expect to get the goss secondhand. Anyway, laters, dude. Some of us got stuff to do."

They hung up, and Rufus finally got to put his other arm in his sweater. He jogged downstairs, where he found Michael, Dad, and Noah in the hall, putting the finishing touches to a Lego tower that was so high, Noah had to sit on Michael's shoulders to put the last bricks on. Rufus frowned. "Have we *got* that much Lego?"

"Oh, you can never have too much Lego," Dad said vaguely, which probably meant he'd been buying up half of Toys"R"Us again. Michael winced, even though it'd been *years* since Dad had last used Lego as an offensive weapon and it was way past time he got over it. "Are you off, then?" Dad asked.

"Yep," Michael answered, handing Noah over to Dad. "See you later, shorty."

Noah mumbled something into Dad's neck.

Dad patted his back. "Yes, they're coming back. Don't worry."

Broke Rufus's heart, like, *every time*.

Michael nudged him. "Come on, then, are we going out or what?"

They stepped out of the B&B into pale sunshine and hardly a breath of wind. It was a Saturday, so Sandown was as busy as it ever got in the winter, which was not very. It felt weird, being somewhere so quiet, after the bustle of Southampton. The island was a great place to visit, Rufus thought, but he wouldn't want to live here. He smiled.

"What are you grinning about?" Michael demanded. "Have I got something on my face?"

"I was just thinking about stuff. You know. Me moving off the island, getting qualified, getting a proper job, all that stuff. Might never have happened if it hadn't been for you." Rufus blinked a bit quicker than usual.

"Oi, no slushy stuff. Just cos it's our anniversary don't mean you get to turn into a girl and bawl your eyes out."

"Dare you to say that in front of Liz and Trix. Go on, I dare you."

"Do I look like a man with a death wish?"

"Sometimes, yes. Like that time I'd worked a twelve-hour shift until 2 a.m. and you woke me up at six for sex."

Michael smirked. "Made it worth your while, though, didn't I?"

Yes, Rufus recalled. Yes, he had.

They walked down the slipway, along the prom, and up to the pier, where they hurried through the indoor bits with their raucous cacophony of slot machines and video games—Michael's word-of-the-day calendar had become an annual tradition, and Rufus had to admit it was good for the vocabulary. Getting out of the dimly lit amusements bit and into the bright fresh air again, Rufus drew in a deep breath. "You know, I'm sure the sea smells different here than in Southampton. I mean, I know it's like the *same* sea, but it still smells different somehow. Saltier. And more seaweedy."

"Yeah, there's more engine oil in Southampton waters." Michael sounded a bit distracted. "You got the docks there, but out here, it's all clear water till you hit France."

"We should go back to France." Rufus slipped his hand in Michael's as they walked up the pier through all the doughnut stalls and assorted seaside larks, closed now for the winter.

"So you can trick me into eating snails again?"

"You *liked* the snails. And the *moules*. And the oysters." Rufus grinned at the memory. "I liked you liking the oysters."

"I don't need oysters to get me in the mood," Michael said with a leer.

Rufus let go of Michael's hand to give his arse a surreptitious squeeze, just as they got to the steps that led down to the serious end of the pier.

"Oi, no funny business. I know I'm irresistible, but we're out in public here." Michael glanced around and smirked. "Even if it is just a couple of sad old men with their rods out, playing with their tackle."

"Don't be rude about the fishermen. Unless you want to find out what a fish feels like when it gets a hook in the lip."

There were only a couple of them there, both with hats pulled down over their eyes. Neither had reacted to Michael's words, which more or less confirmed Rufus's strong suspicion they were asleep. For all intents and purposes, Rufus and Michael were alone here. It made it more romantic, somehow.

Rufus leaned over the end of the pier to look down at the water. "Just think, if there'd been sharks around here four years ago today, my whole life could've been different."

"Oi, what about mine?"

"Yours would've just been a lot shorter. And messier. And you'd definitely have made the front page of the *County Post*. But what if you'd said yes when Trix proposed? That would've been even *worse*."

"Thanks. Nice to know you'd rather see me torn apart by sharks than married to someone else."

"I *meant*, it would've messed up Liz's life too. And Trix's, obviously."

"Really know how to make a bloke feel good about himself, don't you?"

"Mm, I'll make you feel good later," Rufus purred. "What do you reckon—is this the spot you dived in from? They still haven't done a proper job of fixing that chain. I'm amazed nobody's sued them." It'd basically been tied up with a piece of by now very weathered string.

"Yep," Michael mused, wandering over to join him. "It was right over there where Trix proposed. I can even remember the words she used. 'Babes, I love you so much, will you marry me?'"

Rufus nodded.

Michael grinned. "So is it a yes, or what?"

"What?"

"You wanna get hitched, or what?"

Rufus stared at him. "Let me get this straight. You just asked me to marry you with a *secondhand proposal*?"

Michael just shrugged, still with that smug smile on his stupidly handsome face.

Rufus took a step back, narrowing his eyes. "So you want history to repeat itself, do you? Well, two can play at that game."

He took a deep breath and ran straight at Michael, arms outstretched.

It didn't *quite* go according to plan. Yes, he managed to impact Michael with a fair amount of force, but somehow Michael managed to grab hold and not let go. Which meant both of them went sailing over the edge when the chain gave way.

There was barely time to think *oh shit* before he hit the water. It was bloody *freezing*, and sucked him under for several seconds before spitting him out again. Rufus gasped for breath as he surfaced, flailing. Beside him, Michael's dark head broke the water.

He was *laughing*.

"You *tosser*," Rufus spluttered, then couldn't help laughing too.

"What?" Michael demanded, slinging an arm around Rufus that almost pushed him under again. "Hey, we're in this together, right? Where you go, I go." He paused for a splutter as a particularly right-thinking wave slapped him in the face. "And the other way around, yeah? Together for life. So what's your answer—you gonna marry me or what?"

Well, it was *sort* of romantic. And it was very Michael. "You're a total git. And yes, I'll marry you. Now get me back on dry land and out of these wet clothes."

Michael pulled him close and pressed a wet, salty kiss to his lips.

Rufus took a moment to savour the warm, mushy feelings inside him, all the warmer for the contrast with the cold, soggy feelings of his outsides.

Then he put a hand on Michael's head and ducked him under.

Dear Reader,

Thank you for reading JL Merrow's *Lovers Leap*!

We know your time is precious and you have many, many entertainment options, so it means a lot that you've chosen to spend your time reading. We really hope you enjoyed it.

We'd be honored if you'd consider posting a review—good or bad—on sites like **Amazon, Barnes & Noble, Kobo, Goodreads, Twitter, Facebook, Tumblr,** and your blog or website. We'd also be honored if you told your friends and family about this book. Word of mouth is a book's lifeblood!

For more information on upcoming releases, author interviews, blog tours, contests, giveaways, and more, please sign up for our weekly, spam-free newsletter and visit us around the web:

Newsletter: tinyurl.com/RiptideSignup
Twitter: twitter.com/RiptideBooks
Facebook: facebook.com/RiptidePublishing
Goodreads: tinyurl.com/RiptideOnGoodreads
Tumblr: riptidepublishing.tumblr.com

Thank you so much for Reading the Rainbow!

RiptidePublishing.com

ALSO BY JL MERROW

It's All Geek to Me
Damned If You Do
Pricks and Pragmatism
Camwolf
Muscling Through
Wight Mischief
Midnight in Berlin
Hard Tail
Slam!
Fall Hard
Raising the Rent
To Love a Traitor
Sex, Lies and Edelweiss
Trick of Time
Snared

The Plumber's Mate Mysteries
Pressure Head
Relief Valve
Heat Trap
Blow Down (July 2016)

The Shamwell Tales
Caught!
Played!
Out!

The Midwinter Manor Series
Poacher's Fall
Keeper's Pledge

ABOUT THE AUTHOR

JL Merrow is that rare beast, an English person who refuses to drink tea. She read Natural Sciences at Cambridge, where she learned many things, chief amongst which was that she never wanted to see the inside of a lab ever again. Her one regret is that she never mastered the ability of punting one-handed whilst holding a glass of champagne.

She writes across genres, with a preference for contemporary gay romance and the paranormal, and is frequently accused of humour. Her novella *Muscling Through* was a 2013 EPIC Award finalist, and her novel *Slam!* won the 2013 Rainbow Award for Best LGBT Romantic Comedy.

JL Merrow is a member of the UK GLBTQ Fiction Meet (ukglbtfictionmeet.co.uk) organizing team.

Find JL Merrow online at: jlmerrow.com, Twitter as @jlmerrow, and Facebook at facebook.com/jl.merrow.

Enjoy more stories like
Lovers Leap
at RiptidePublishing.com!

Too Stupid to Live
ISBN: 978-1-937551-85-8

With This Bling
ISBN: 978-1-62649-360-5

Earn Bonus Bucks!

Earn 1 Bonus Buck for each dollar you spend. Find out how at
RiptidePublishing.com/news/bonus-bucks.

Win Free Ebooks for a Year!

Pre-order coming soon titles directly through our site and you'll
receive one entry into a drawing for a chance to win free books for
a year! Get the details at RiptidePublishing.com/contests.

CPSIA information can be obtained at www.ICGtesting.com
Printed in the USA
LVOW07s1544110316

478795LV00005B/484/P